CRASH LANDING

PUBLIC PRESSURE, PRIVATE PAIN

Dale Hunter is fighting to save his business from disaster in the rapidly evolving technology world of the 1990s when his business associate, who is also in dire circumstances after a recent business failure and in the middle of a vicious divorce battle, is found dead in his office in an apparent suicide. The police immediately report it as a suspicious death, possibly murder. They discover connections to organised crime and a multitude of potential motives for murder and start investigating a widening web of likely suspects—including Dale Hunter.

The threat of murder charges adds to Hunter's challenges with his business troubles and the family trauma of his wife's recent breast cancer diagnosis. The murder investigation then reveals the victim's connections to organised crime and it suddenly gets more complicated and more dangerous for Dale Hunter. Who did what? Why? How? And who will die next? The only way out for Hunter is to find the answers to those questions before he becomes the next victim.

EARLY REVIEWS:

"Right away I love how we're firmly grounded in the who, what, and where. I also love the way you pepper the basic descriptions of the scene with interiority from Dale and background information on what he's doing and why, and to get it doled out in bursts rather than dumps makes for a compelling reading experience. Additionally, you drive home the tough economic climate that Dale is up against. That sense of opposition and stakes draws us in further and gets us to actually care about Dale Hunter. Nice work!" - Kenneth Zink, New York.

Crash Landing starts well with a suspicious death. And Dale is at the centre of it as a suspect! The secondary characters are interesting. Dale tries to save his company… Good chapter endings. The pace picks up nicely after a good twist that I didn't see coming. More good twists and turns throughout. Not a mean feat!! - Patricia Lavoie, Montreal.

Public pressure, private pain.

A
DALE HUNTER
THRILLER

CRASH LANDING

DELVIN CHATTERSON

Thank you
for joining!
the adventure!
Del.

THE DALE HUNTER THRILLER SERIES

NO EASY MONEY - *You never win playing by the rules...* First in the series of Dale Hunter Crime Thriller novels, an explosive mix of crime, cash and computers in the 1980s. Entrepreneurs face challenges every day. It's hard to be a hero. Dale Hunter is facing threats from the Montreal Mafia and dirty dealing by crooked business associates. He wants to survive and not play by gangster rules. It will require courage and creativity and the support of some new friends. Somebody is going to get killed.

SIMPLY THE BEST - *It may be simple, it's never easy* Dale Hunter is again up against the gangsters who tried to murder him once and are now threatening his family. Meanwhile, Hunter's new partner in Taiwan is dragging him into smuggling schemes with the Triads. The danger escalates. Hunter's escape may be simple, but it's never easy.

MERGER MANIAC - *Some offers have to be refused* Dale Hunter is trying to save his business from competitive threats in the rapidly evolving computer business of the 1980s. He's looking for partners when he's suddenly approached by the Mafia to participate in their money laundering schemes. Hunter has to walk a dangerous tightrope to avoid getting dragged into more crime and corruption.

BAD BOYS IN BOSTON - *It's just business, never personal* Thirty years after fighting crime and corruption in the 1980s, Dale Hunter and Frank the Fixer are now drawn into rescuing a niece kidnapped into sex trafficking and online pornography by Russian gangsters in Boston. Dale and Frank follow a treacherous trail into the dangerous and violent international sex trade that also exposes Frank's tragic family history in Africa and more violent threats closer to home in Montreal.

CRASH LANDING - *Public pressure, private pain* Dale Hunter is fighting to save his business from disaster, when his business associate is found dead in an apparent suicide. The police immediately report it as a suspicious death, possibly murder. They pursue a widening web of likely suspects, including Dale Hunter. Then connections to organised crime are revealed and it suddenly gets more complicated and more dangerous. The only way out is to find the truth before Hunter becomes the next victim.

WHATEVER IT TAKES – *Trust nobody* Dale Hunter is shocked to discover that his friend and longtime mentor and role model entrepreneur, is a ruthless, greedy and ambitious egotist, probably crooked, and possibly a murderer. Hunter is persuaded to help extricate his friend from the dirty deals with criminals manipulating local politicians for profit in major construction projects. Instead of running for cover, Hunter gets drawn into the lethal conspiracies himself.

HIGH PRAISE FOR THE DALE HUNTER SERIES

"Chatterson's language conveys mayhem with a brevity that practically demands attention. Action sequences are rapid fire and corrosive … offset by threatening undertones. Chatterson pens crime drama that is fast-paced and involved." INDIE READER REVIEW

"Great read! … I had to get up in the middle of the night to finish it!" Ken Collins (Canada)

"I read this book in one day … How do I get my hands on his next book?" Margaret Heaton (USA)

Amazing! An absolutely outstanding writer! Hooked and thoroughly entertained. …. a captivating author." Peter J. Malouf (Canada)

"I liked it a lot! And I was there, in the computer business of the 1980s. I'm telling all my friends, very impressive!" Gilles Gaudet (Canada)

"Welcome to the '80s Business World. I love how the story flowed and the intensity continued to increase, keeping you reading to the very end. Keeps you on the edge of your seat for an intense and exciting read. Enjoy the ride! It's a fast one!" Amanda Leeber (USA), Amazon.com Review

"Loved it right from the beginning! The passion between the characters had me not wanting to put it down. A definite must read! Looking forward to reading book two." Jasmin Moore, Goodreads Reviewer

EARLY REVIEWS OF BAD BOYS IN BOSTON

"Intriguing, scary, occasionally disturbing." "Kept me reading every page."

"A story that needs to be told and Chatterson meets the challenge in his latest exciting and entertaining Dale Hunter Series action thriller."

"I love the concept of jumping forward 30 years in the series and how the crimefighting sidekick becomes the hero! It's even more fascinating to learn that Frank the Fixer, the troubled young Somalian refugee to Montreal, now a tough-guy PI, is based on a Somalian colleague of Del's from the 1980s!"

DEL CHATTERSON IS ALSO *YOUR UNCLE RALPH,*
WITH ADVICE FOR ENTREPRENEURS

READER REVIEWS:
THE COMPLETE DO-IT-YOURSELF GUIDE TO BUSINESS PLANS

Get the results you want!
Everything you need to know from Start-up to Exit.

4.5 Stars on Amazon

"Comprehensive and thorough, for a bullet proof business plan."
"Very informative and helpful for any aspiring Entrepreneur."
*"Not boring. For a solid business plan and to avoid basic mistakes
when starting a business."*

DON'T DO IT THE HARD WAY
AVOID THE SEVEN BIGGEST MISTAKES THAT ENTREPRENEURS MAKE

5 Stars on Amazon

"Great book. Well written and an easy read."
A wealth of business experience distilled into easy-to-understand lessons."
*I liked his chapter on Managing in Difficult times - Stay focused, be relevant,
look for opportunities in the crisis and leverage it to create urgency."*
*"I would strongly recommend this book, most importantly, for learning
from other's mistakes.*
A very good read and really great advice."
"We can immediately apply these ideas and keep on fixing what has to be fixed."
*"Very complete and comprehensive, whether for the start-up entrepreneur,
or small business people at any stage of their careers."*
*I like the format - a great approach to get important lessons across - worthy
of being reviewed regularly to assure that your ideas, strategies and tactics
are being implemented."*
*"Great information and the stories are a bonus. For someone like me
that is going to start-up a business this book gives you the push you need."*
Stop shopping and buy this book now."

Public pressure, private pain.

A DALE HUNTER THRILLER

CRASH LANDING

DELVIN CHATTERSON

CRASH LANDING

PUBLIC PRESSURE, PRIVATE PAIN.

DELVIN CHATTERSON

ISBN 978-0-9879569-9-6 Print SC
ISBN 978-1-0689279-0-4 E-Book

Disclaimer: *Some of the events, individuals, businesses and institutions in this novel are real, the story and the primary characters are entirely fiction. Any apparent use of real names or similarity to real people is purely coincidental.*

Published by:
Uncle Ralph's Publishing Empire
(Division of 146152 Canada Inc.)

&

———————————————

Dedicated to enlightened entrepreneurs everywhere,
trying to do better for themselves and their families, their
employees, customers, and business partners while meeting
their obligations to local communities, their nation,
and the planet.

Also dedicated with gratitude to the families, friends, and
lovers of entrepreneurs for their support and understanding.

PART 1

WE'RE GOING DOWN!

1.

Dale Hunter was in his large corner office at 3D Computer Products, hunched over the paperwork spread out on his desk. Through the window in the dark behind him he could hear the rush-hour traffic fading away on the autoroute with the swoosh and rumble of cars and transport trucks. The intermittent thump and bump of vehicles on the rough service-road between the autoroute and the parking lot echoed off the front of the low industrial building where his offices and warehouse were located. There were only a few lights on in the offices.

Hunter held his head in his hands. *How the hell did this happen? Almost ten years of flying high, now I'm trying to avoid a crash landing. What a fucking disaster.*

How the hell did this happen? What did I do wrong?

It was quiet in the office as all of the staff had gone home for the day. Dale was alone, except for his business associate, Bobbie Brydon, who was working in another spacious executive office on the other side of the front reception area, and Brydon's daughter, Lisa, in a smaller office down the hall and around the corner from her father. Brydon had also run a computer products distribution business and was now working with Dale to help him take 3D Computers in a new direction and avoid the disaster of a decline into oblivion. Dale had made a deal with Brydon to work in his offices temporarily. Lisa was part of the deal. It was a complicated story and Dale was still trying to manage it to a happy ending.

He looked up at his computer screen, then at the printouts and financial statements spread out in front of him before dropping his head back in his hands. He squeezed his eyes shut and clenched his jaw.

The 1980s had been a very good decade in the personal computer business, but this was 1993 and times had changed. Dale had started from zero after leaving a senior executive position at a multi-national computer manufacturing business in Montreal. He'd started his own business to import and distribute computer products to retailers delivering personal computers to offices, homes, and schoolrooms everywhere. In less than ten years, his business had grown to thirty-five million dollars a year in sales. He had fifty-five employees located in sales offices and distribution centres in Montreal, Toronto, Calgary, Vancouver and Boston.

However, in spite of his skill at building and managing the business, Dale was not sheltered from the brutal restructuring of the rapidly evolving computer industry in the early 1990s. It might even destroy his business. The big players in the industry were steadily getting stronger and more dominant by eliminating all the annoying small business competitors and by merging with their rivals in order to lower their costs and expand their market share. Revenue growth was slowing as personal computers seemed to have been installed on every desktop in every home, office, and school in North America. The surviving businesses were now battling each other in a declining personal computer market and trying to meet the continuously changing demands for newer technology.

Prospects for the survival of 3D Computer Products were not looking good. Dale had reluctantly reduced staff and cut operating expenses, but reviewing his current financial statements provided a painful reminder that drastic measures were still required. Major suppliers were waiting for overdue payments; customer receipts were getting slower; the bank was threatening to withdraw its support.

How did this happen? Dale was distressed, looking for answers, and trying to understand how he could find a way out. *Was I too arrogant? Blind to the warning signs? Over-confident? Naïve? Not as smart as I thought I was? Fuck! There's no way out ....*

This must be when business owners give up and decide to just end it and kill themselves.

He turned his attention back to his paperwork.

BANG! What was that?

Dale looked up at the sound that had interrupted his thoughts. *That sounded like a gunshot.* He frowned. *No way. Maybe a truck backfiring out on the highway. Anyway, enough of this worrying about what went wrong. I've got to stop bitching and moaning and get back to work on some solutions.*

He looked at his watch and saw it was seven-thirty.

Susan and the kids would already have given up waiting on him. They'd have had supper without him by now. It wasn't the first time. He could have worked at home after supper, but this evening he needed access to the office computers to crunch the numbers one more time. He decided he'd leave soon and ask Bobbie and Lisa to leave with him, since they didn't have their own keys or codes to the security system.

He suddenly heard footsteps running toward his office and someone screaming.

"Dale! Dale! Help me! My dad's shot himself!"

He jumped up from his desk and met Lisa in the hallway. She was frantic and in tears. She stopped when she saw him.

"Come quick, Dale! Help me, please. I think he's dead!"

They rushed back together across the reception area and down the hall on the left to Bobbie's office. They stopped in the open doorway.

It was an ugly scene.

Bobbie was lying back in his chair with his head tilted awkwardly to the left. Blood was running from a wound at his right temple across his cheek. The blood was dripping from his chin into his shirt collar. His round belly was thrust forward in the chair, his feet splayed out under the desk in front of him.

His right arm dangled above a handgun lying on the floor.

Dale held Lisa back in the doorway and took two steps forward to look closer and confirm the obvious. Brydon's open eyes stared blankly at the ceiling. There was no exit wound on the other side of his head, but Bobbie Brydon was definitely dead.

"Come with me," Dale said firmly, as he turned back toward a distraught Lisa. He closed the door to Brydon's office and guided her back toward the reception area. He directed her to sit down in one of the black leather armchairs facing the high countertop in front of the receptionist's desk.

He sat down beside her and turned to look at her closely. She was trying to calm herself with deep, slow breaths. The colour had drained from her face and left her with a pale expression of devastation.

Dale said, "I'm sorry, Lisa, so sorry. I'll take care of this. Please, take a few minutes and sit here, try to calm yourself. I'll call 9-1-1 and we can wait together for the ambulance." He squeezed her arm and waited for her to nod.

"Then you should call your mother," he said. "Or I can drive you to see her if you want to tell her about this yourself."

Lisa sat up and quickly shook her head.

"No, no, not my mom! … Oh God. My dad is dead! … Now what do I do?"

Dale was aware of the strained relationship between Lisa and her parents during their long, acrimonious divorce battle that had escalated in the past few months. He stood, patted her gently on the shoulder, and said, "I'm sorry, Lisa. This is going to be hard. I'll help you through it as best I can. There's nothing we can do for Bobbie now. Try to calm yourself and wait here. I'll call for help."

He watched her sit back, straighten up, and take another long slow breath. She looked up at him and nodded. Dale walked over to the reception desk and around to the other side where he could keep an eye on Lisa. He lifted the phone out of the cradle to make the call.

2.

Two uniformed police officers arrived in a blue-and-white police car marked *SPVM - Service de Police de la Ville de Montréal*. They introduced themselves as Cloutier and Dubé and said they were responding to the 9-1-1 call from a Mr. Dale Hunter. Dale confirmed he had made the call and introduced them to Lisa Brydon. Cloutier wrote their names in his notebook before switching from French to English and asking, "So what happened here?"

Dale explained, "There were just the three of us here working late, when we heard a shot and Lisa found her father dead in his office. You can see for yourself. He's in the first office on your left." He pointed down the hall toward Brydon's office. "I closed the door, but it's not locked."

He sat down again beside Lisa as the two officers went down the hall. After waiting quietly together for a while, Dale left briefly and came back with two glasses of water which he set on the low square table in front of them. He was lost in thought and took another moment to arrange the magazines on the table in orderly stacks with the titles showing. Then he took the day's newspapers off the table to put them in the recycling bin beside the receptionist's desk before dropping back into the armchair beside Lisa. He could be a bit obsessive about neatness, constantly rearranging things around him, but he found it a calming distraction.

While they waited, they heard the police officers down the hall talking to each other and then on the radio to someone else. The ambulance from *Urgence Santé* arrived shortly after the police with its bright lights flashing. The two paramedics in orange vests, carrying their gear, came in and were also directed by Dale down the hall to Brydon's office. After a few minutes, they returned and went back out to the ambulance, turned off the amber flashers and sat waiting in the parking lot under the lights out front.

It was a good half-hour before Dale heard the two officers coming back toward them. He glanced at Lisa. "Are you OK?" She nodded and looked up at the officers arriving in the reception area.

"We'd like to ask you a few more questions," said Cloutier. "Mr. Hunter, can you go to your office and wait for us there, please. Officer Dubé and I would like to speak to Miss Brydon first, since she was the one to find her father like that." He glanced at his notebook. "Your name's Lisa, right?"

She nodded.

The younger officer, Dubé, smiled at Lisa and tried to look friendly. He pulled out two armchairs on either side of the low table so they could sit facing her. Dale stood and said, "Is that OK, Lisa, or do you want me to stay here?"

She looked up at Dale, then at the two officers. "I'm fine," she said. "I can handle it."

Outside the windows, Dale noticed the flashing amber lights go on again and the ambulance pulled forward to leave the parking lot and go out the driveway onto the service road heading east into the city. He looked at Cloutier. "Why is the ambulance leaving?"

"This is not an emergency," said Cloutier. "I guess they're needed somewhere else. Like you said to the dispatch, *le monsieur est mort*. The gentleman is dead. They checked for us and made it official. But we called it in as a suspicious death, so now we have to wait for the investigators to arrive and inspect the scene before we can have the body removed." He looked down at Lisa, still slumped in the armchair. "Sorry, but we'll need to keep you here a little while longer."

Dale frowned. "What do you mean suspicious death? It seems obvious to me," he said. "Not suspicious at all. He shot himself in the head. We found him exactly like that." He tilted his head toward Brydon's office, then looked at Lisa. "You didn't see anything suspicious did you, Lisa?"

She quickly shook her head.

"Maybe obvious to you," said Cloutier, "but I've got to do my job and be sure about what happened here. We have a violent death and no witnesses. No suicide note. I called for detectives to come and check it out. They're the experts and they'll bring a forensic technician to analyze the scene and collect the evidence. We just have a few more questions for you, while we wait for them."

"Can I call my wife first?" asked Dale.

Cloutier hesitated before replying. He looked at Dubé, who shrugged. Cloutier said, "Yes, go ahead. *Pas de problème.*

No reason not to call your wife. Maybe don't tell her too much until you get home."

Dale looked back at him thinking he didn't need any advice on what to say to his wife. He heard Dubé asking Lisa for her full name, home address, and telephone number. He reached over the reception counter and removed his business card from the holder on the desk and handed it to Cloutier. "My phone numbers are there. The mobile phone is installed in my car so that number's not much use unless I'm on the road."

"I'll need your home address and phone number too," said Cloutier.

Dale took the card and picked up a pen off the reception counter to write the information on the back and handed it again to Cloutier. "I'll wait for you in my office," he said. "It's down the hallway, first office on the right." He looked at Lisa who nodded to him, then he left to call his wife, Susan.

3.

Seated back in his office, Dale called and told Susan not to wait up for him. "There's been … uh, an accident at the office." She had asked if he was all right and he reassured her. "I'm fine. But it's complicated … I'll tell you more when I get home." As he'd guessed, she and the kids had already had supper and the kids had gone to bed. It reminded him he needed to grab a drink and a sandwich from the vending machines in the lunchroom before Cloutier came to his office for more questions.

Twenty minutes later, after Cloutier was done asking his questions, Dale returned with him to the front entrance and sat back down with Lisa just as the forensic investigator arrived carrying two large cases and a camera slung over his shoulder. He was a tall, slim young man with large black-rimmed glasses, in jeans and a checkered short-sleeve shirt, who hadn't taken the time to comb his hair or put on a suit and tie for the late evening call from his home. He stopped at reception to put down two cases and a camera and throw his light jacket over a chair. He pulled out a neatly folded white lab coat from one of the cases, shook it out and shrugged it on. Then he removed a pair of blue surgical gloves and put them on before grabbing the two cases and camera to follow Cloutier and Dubé back down the hall to Brydon's office. He placed the cases in the hallway outside the office door and then did a full assessment of the scene, taking photographs, and writing notes on his clipboard.

Lisa watched the officers and the investigator coming and going, but she remained seated patiently at reception. Between interruptions, she slouched in the chair with a vacant gaze directed at the floor in front of her. The two glasses of water, one half empty, were still on the table. Dale asked if she'd like a fresh cup of coffee and a sandwich or anything from the lunchroom. She shook her head.

"I'll top up your glass of water at least," said Dale. He reached for it and added, "We might have to wait a while yet. I'm going to get a coffee and a muffin, and I can bring you something, if you like."

She shook her head again. "No thanks, I'm fine."

Dale came back with his coffee and muffin to sit beside her. He was getting impatient and anxious to know what was happening and how long this would take. Then the two detectives who had been called arrived at the front door and walked into reception. They were both in suits. The older, heavier one in a wrinkled grey suit jacket with his tie pulled loose at the neck had probably combed his hair at some point during the day, but it had still not settled down for him. He didn't appear to care about his hair or his rumpled appearance. Dale recognized him immediately as Detective Claude Samson, whom he had met during previous investigations into Dale's encounters with organised crime.

Why would he get the call to check on an apparent suicide?

The other detective was younger, more fit and neater, with a dark blue suit and patterned blue tie pulled up to the collar of his white button-down shirt. They introduced themselves with a brief nod. Dale got no special attention or acknowledgement of his prior meetings with Samson. The two detectives were directed to Brydon's office where Cloutier and Dubé had remained with the investigator.

They spent about half an hour there with the two officers and the investigator before coming back to reception where they confirmed with Dale and Lisa what they had seen for themselves and learned from the officers and the investigator. The younger detective, introduced as Pat Carney, read from his notes and asked them to clarify a few points on who was where and what they were doing when they heard the shot.

Samson then asked Dale to show them around the premises and he asked the young investigator to join them for the tour of 3D Computer Products. They started in reception with a few flash photos, then they went back down the hall past Brydon's open office door and glanced in at the scene where Cloutier and Dubé were standing in front of Brydon's body at his desk. Lisa had remained at reception and Dale turned away from the doorway to look back quickly where she sat staring at the floor in front of her. They continued around the corner down the short hallway to the right to Lisa's office, where they took more photos from all angles, then continued into the technical services area with its work benches and countertops along the wall and a small office near the entrance to the warehouse which occupied the back of the building.

Dale turned on the lights as they walked into each area and the investigator followed them for more photos. At the entrance to the warehouse, Dale was about to key in the passcode to open the door when Samson stopped him. "Wait a minute, don't touch any more doorknobs until we've had a chance to pick up the fingerprints."

He nodded to the investigator, who said, "OK, I'll do this one now, just a sec." He went back down the hall with the camera slung over his shoulder and returned with his fingerprinting kit. He dusted the doorknob and keypad, before photographing close-ups and removing the prints on tape strips. "Now you can open it," he said to Dale.

Dale tapped the keypad and opened the door to turn on the high ceiling lights. The investigator said, "Hold on a sec and I'll do the light switch too." Again, he dusted and lifted prints from the switch panel, then with his rubber gloves flicked the lights on so they could look down the aisles of shelving and piled boxes of computer products. The investigator stepped inside and took more photos. He walked to the back of the warehouse and looked at the rear doors and the loading dock in the shipping and receiving area. More photos. He came back to the warehouse entrance and said to Dale, "Can you leave the door open and the lights on, please? I'll come back to get more fingerprints around the shipping and receiving door and I'll pick up the outside from around the back after we're done."

Dale was shaking his head at all this effort that seemed like an unnecessary make-work project for the two detectives and their investigator. *They must be getting bonus pay for overtime.* "The warehouse has been closed and locked up since the staff left about five-thirty," he said. "The back door is also on the alarm system, and we have a camera outside. Nobody's been here that shouldn't have been here."

"Then we should soon be able to say so for sure," said Samson. "Just you, Brydon, and his daughter Lisa, since about five-thirty. Is that right?"

"Yes, that's right," said Dale.

"I'll take more photos outside, front and back, before I leave," said the investigator. "It's always better to have too much information than to discover later we missed something significant. I'm sure you don't want the whole building shutdown tomorrow while we process the crime scene. If I finish the building tonight we should be able to close off just the one office the body's in until we're done with all the evidence collected and analyzed."

Dale shrugged. "We need to be able to get back to work here tomorrow morning. So please give us back our offices as soon as you can." He looked at Samson, who was non-committal. They walked back past a conference room behind the front reception area and down the hall past open offices with partitions between the desks and three small, closed offices along the wall before arriving at Dale's larger office with windows facing the front parking lot. Lights were turned on and photos taken as they went.

As the investigator stepped inside to take photos of Dale's office, Samson said, "He'll be looking at all the fingerprints from doorknobs and other surfaces, so we'd like to have yours and Lisa's, if you don't mind. It helps us identify those we know should be here, and we can take a closer look at any we don't recognize."

"Sure," said Dale. "Whatever it takes to get this over with."

A few minutes later, after fingerprinting that included Lisa, who was still waiting patiently in the reception area, Dale was again at his desk with the two detectives seated in front of him. He reached for his coffee and found it nearly empty, but took a sip. It was now cold, so he put it back down on the square blue leather coaster beside his desk blotter.

He spoke to Claude Samson, "We met before, when I was in a jam with the Mafia and you worked in the Organised Crime Unit, remember?"

"Yeah, I remember," said Samson. His tone was not that of an old friend renewing acquaintances.

Dale turned to the younger man in a fresher suit, Detective Pat Carney. "You must work with Detective-Sergeant Hélène Bourassa also. She knows me well. Maybe she can help you guys sort this out to everyone's satisfaction."

Samson was still not looking friendly. He replied, "She saw your name when this was called in and decided to send us. She knows you too well to get involved herself."

"I see," said Dale. "But this should be easy for you anyway. Obviously a suicide, don't you think?" He looked from one detective to the other.

"Maybe too obvious," said Samson. "We'll make sure, though. Satisfy everybody before we're done."

"Alright, let's get this over with," said Dale. "I'd like to get home before midnight and take Lisa home first if she wants me to. I don't think she should be left alone after all this, so I'm trying to persuade her to go to her mother. A hell of an experience for a daughter, to find him like that … dead in his office, with a bullet in his head."

"Right," Samson said. "So what's the story there? Parents split and the daughter sided with her father?"

Dale replied, "It's been hard for her, but I don't think she's taken sides. Caught in the middle, it was pretty nasty. She's tried to mediate between them, I think. She's young, but she's a tough kid. Pushing them to sort it out and finalize the divorce. But it wasn't going anywhere, and his wife was getting more difficult and demanding. She had some high-priced lawyers chasing Bobbie for more than he could handle. He was never going to give her enough to satisfy her and end the battles. I guess he decided to end it his way."

Samson shrugged. "That's one way to end a bad relationship. Not usually the husband who ends up dead, though." He clenched his jaw, thinking of all the domestic abuse and homicides he'd been called on to investigate.

He peered at Hunter. "How about you and Brydon?

Did you get along as partners?"

"He was never my partner," said Dale. "He owed me after his company went belly up and we made a deal for him to work it off. He needed an office and his daughter was here to help him out. They've been here about six months."

Carney asked, "And how was that going?"

"We were making progress."

"Business looks good to me," said Carney. "Lots of money in computers, I hear."

"Used to be," said Dale. "Not so much anymore, business is tough."

Samson interjected, "His daughter says you and Brydon didn't get along that well. Yelling at each other sometimes."

"Bobbie could be an asshole," Dale responded. "He didn't get along with a lot of people, unless they were useful to him. I tolerated him too much, probably. He wasn't accomplishing much for me, so I had to push him a lot. Sometimes it got loud. That was more his style than mine. But if he hollered, I hollered back."

"Lisa tells us she heard you having an argument this evening."

"Yeah, that happened. The usual crap between us. We're both pretty stubborn, sometimes stupid about it."

"And if it wasn't suicide, you were the only other person in the building who could have killed him and gone back to your office before she found him."

"Ha!" Dale was shaking his head. "Interesting theory. But it wasn't me. He did make me mad enough to think of killing him a few times, but not seriously. He was no use to me dead."

Samson scowled at him. "This is serious, Hunter. No time to be joking about killing him. The man is dead and it's not yet so clear that he killed himself. If it wasn't you, who else might have a motive?"

Dale was surprised they were pursuing this line of questioning.

Murdered?

"That might be a long list," said Dale. "Like I said, he could be an asshole. He also ripped-off a lot of people to make money for himself. That leaves a lot of angry people out there. But it seems to me he also had a lot of good reasons to kill himself. He was in a vicious divorce battle with a vindictive wife who wanted to take every last nickel he had and put him out on the street. His company had recently gone bankrupt and a lot of unhappy creditors were still pounding on him to get their money back. Failed marriage and a failed business. Those are pretty good motives for suicide."

Carney spoke up, "Yeah, that's what his daughter said. Apparently, she worried about him with all the stress he was under. She thought he might be depressed and didn't see any way out. She wasn't that surprised that he might decide to commit suicide. Shocked to find him like that, but not surprised."

Samson scowled again at Hunter. "But the asshole you describe doesn't sound like somebody who'd commit suicide. Did he ever give you any indication he might do something like that?"

"No, never. But he was a volatile guy, prone to fits of rage. Maybe he just suddenly lost it and decided to take it out on himself."

Carney leaned forward and asked, "Did you know he had a gun? Have you ever seen it before?"

"No. It never even occurred to me. I never heard him talk of owning a gun."

Carney asked, "Do you keep a gun or any other weapon at the office?"

"Hell, no."

The investigator, still wearing his white lab coat, came to the doorway of Dale's office removing his blue surgical gloves and leaned in. "We're done here," he said. "I've called the morgue to come and pick up the body. I'll give you my initial report with the file first thing tomorrow morning, Claude. See you then, OK?"

Samson nodded to him and turned to Dale. "We'll leave an officer here until the morgue takes the body away. Then he'll seal off Brydon's office before he leaves. We need to keep everyone out of there until we're finished the investigation."

"That'll be a nice welcome to the office tomorrow morning," said Dale. "I'll lock it up after you all leave tonight and then make sure I'm the first one here tomorrow morning to explain what's happened. How long will your investigation take before we can have Brydon's office back."

"We'll need a few days before we can release it." said Samson. "We'll call if we have any more questions or we have to come back." He got up to leave and added, "Thanks for your help. Give our sympathies to Lisa and her mother."

Dale ushered them back through reception and out the front door. They both nodded to Lisa without a further word. Dale returned to sit down beside her again and explain what was happening next.

"Do you want to wait for me until they're done here? Then I can take you to your mother."

Lisa took a moment to collect herself. "Yes, please. I think that's best. It might help if you're there when I tell her about this. Thank you, Dale"

She gave him a faint smile before the pale sadness returned to her face.

4.

Susan was asleep when Dale got home, it was after one in the morning. He went straight to bed but didn't sleep well and was up again before six. Susan came downstairs later, looking dishevelled and disgruntled and found him at the kitchen counter on the wall phone speaking to his office manager, Marie de Carlo. He glanced at Susan and gave her a quick smile, raising one finger to indicate he wouldn't be long on the phone.

"Yes, Marie," he said, "I'll tell you more when I see you. I'll try to get to the office soon, before you or anyone else gets there."

As soon as he hung up, Susan said, "You're home late and leaving again already? I wanted to talk to you. I waited up for you last night but gave up and went to bed when you still weren't home at eleven. What happened?"

"Yeah, sorry. Thanks for leaving my dinner in the fridge last night."

He came around the counter and gave her a brief hug and a kiss on the cheek. He directed her to a stool to sit beside him at the counter and then sat facing her with his elbow beside his coffee cup and the half-finished bowl of cereal. "Do you want a coffee yourself?"

"No, I'll have my tea later. Just tell me what's going on."

"Yeah, let's talk about it, but I do have to get to the office soon." Dale apologized for not explaining over the phone last night and then told her about Bobbie Brydon killing himself at the office and the police having to investigate what they called a suspicious death. "For some reason they're thinking he might not have killed himself. It seemed obvious to me and Lisa when we found him dead at his desk, but the first two officers who arrived still had questions about it, so they called for detectives to come and investigate. It took a while for them to do all that, taking photos and fingerprints everywhere, before they removed the body and let us all go home."

Susan was shocked but listened attentively. Wide-eyed, she held her hand to her mouth. "My God, Dale," she said, "that's horrible. Why would he kill himself at your office? And poor Lisa, finding him like that."

"I know. She was pretty shaken up. I didn't think she should go home alone. She had to tell her mother too, so I needed to take her there when we were finally done at the office."

Susan was shaking her head, imagining the scene at the office, then Lisa telling her mother what had happened. She knew them both and had some affection for Lisa but none at all for her mother, Donna Brydon. The word *bitch* kept coming to mind. Susan was too polite to use stronger language for how she really felt about her. The whole Brydon family had been an unnecessary burden for Dale, she thought. Managing the business through a difficult period was already enough strain on him and his family.

"That guy has been nothing but trouble for you," she said. "I don't know why you ever got mixed up with him in the first place, and you kept on trying to work with him."

"Yeah, well, it's over now. He was always hard to work with and he never did help me much. I still have all the challenges in the business to deal with ... explaining a suicide in the office wasn't one of them ... until last night."

Susan nodded to herself and said, "You better get back to the office and be there before the others arrive." She got off her stool. "I have some other news, but you don't have time now. We can talk later."

"Sure," said Dale, "Let's do that. I won't be late tonight. What's up? Good news about the kids, or more problems?"

"Don't worry about it for now. Go."

She left the kitchen and went to get Sean and Keira up for breakfast before school.

5.

In the car on the way to the office, Dale tried to focus on the business issues he still had to deal with. He knew the suicide was going to be a big distraction, especially for the first few hours this morning. Nobody would be able to ignore the yellow police tape in a big X across the closed door of Brydon's office.

Was he still in there? Somebody was sure to ask.

Dale could reassure them they didn't have to worry about a body lying in the office. He had seen Brydon being taken out on a stretcher in a body bag by the morgue attendants last night, before he left with Lisa to go to her mother.

His mind wandered back to worrying about 3D Computers and what he had to do before the company ended up in a body bag. *Shit, that's a terrible image. My business getting hauled off to the morgue. Forget it, that's not gonna happen. Anyway, it'll be more like pulling survivors out of a train wreck if I don't find a way to keep it on the rails. Goddamn Brydon, he wasn't helping much and now his suicide is a big distraction from what I really need to focus on.*

He wondered about Susan's news. He'd recently been thinking he might have to ask her to come back to the office to help out. She'd done that before, when he was just getting started in the business and couldn't afford all the administrative support he needed. With the recent cutbacks he was back at that point again. *I hope she hasn't taken on another commitment and won't have time for me. Is there a problem I don't know about? Keira never has any problems at school, but Sean sometimes needs a little help to stay on the rails.*

He took a moment and tried to put it all in perspective. *It's hard to keep the family a priority with all this shit going on. Tonight I'll make time for them.*

Then his thoughts turned to Brydon's family. *Now there was a never-ending train wreck.*

The scene at the big house on the hillside in Westmount last night was sad and distressing. Dale and Lisa arrived at Brydon's stone mansion on the darkened street near midnight and went up the walk illuminated by a streetlight behind them and the bright lamps on either side of the marbled arch above the front door. Lisa looked back at Dale, who had stopped and waited at the bottom of the broad flagstone steps. She took a deep breath, then leaned on the doorbell. She stepped back for a moment, then pressed it hard again for several seconds.

It wasn't long before they heard yelling inside. "I'm coming! I'm coming! Who is it?" There was movement at the narrow leaded window beside the door and Donna Brydon's face appeared. She looked out at Lisa on the doorstep, then backed away from the window and opened the door. She stood there in a dark-blue nightie wrapped in a white silk housecoat, dyed blond hair in a mess.

"Lisa, what are you doing here at this time of night?"

Then she saw Dale standing on the walk at the bottom of the front steps.

"What's he doing here?"

There was a long pause as Lisa stared at her mother, silently gulping back her emotions before she burst into tears. "Oh, my God, Mommy! Daddy killed himself! At Dale's office tonight."

Donna clapped a hand over her mouth in shock. She backed away from the door to let them in and waved Dale forward to come up the steps. He waited on the top step as Brydon's wife and daughter clenched each other in a fierce embrace. Donna took Lisa's hand and said, "Come in. Tell me what happened."

Dale remained at the door. "I don't think you need me here anymore," he said. Donna turned back to nod at him, then closed the door in his face.

He had walked away and started the long drive back past the office to his home in the West Island. In the quiet calm of a late-night drive across the city, he thought about poor Lisa, already in the middle of an ugly divorce; now she was dealing with a difficult mother right after finding her father had killed himself.

But she's a tough young lady. Smart and ambitious like her father and probably wants to be a rich bitch in Westmount like her mother. She's used to the first-class lifestyle and wants it to continue, I'm sure. Maybe trade up from her little white Mazda Miata to a big Mercedes convertible like her mother's.

Maybe something even more flashy like her father's red Porsche. Those plans were already in jeopardy with a divorce and a bankruptcy affecting her prospects. Now she'll have to figure out how to manage without her father.

When Dale arrived back at the office the next morning, both the Mazda and the Porsche were still sitting in the parking lot. No one else was there yet.

6.

While Dale was busy at the office that morning reassuring his staff about the death of Bobbie Brydon, Lisa and her mother were seated in the breakfast nook at Brydon's house in Westmount, sipping coffee and talking about the family tragedy. Trying to speak of the unspeakable, averting their eyes from each other. Their small white plates covered in toast crumbs had been pushed aside on the table.

"I know it's terrible that he killed himself," said Donna, "but this actually makes it easier for you and me, Lisa. Now we can settle our family affairs without all the expensive mess of a divorce settlement. And you don't have to take sides anymore."

"I wasn't taking sides! I told you, I was trying to help. Daddy was never going to come up with the money you wanted. You've already got everything he ever owned. You could have settled by now and let us all get on with our lives!"

"He didn't deserve a settlement. The bastard cheated on me. And he stole from me and my family. Maybe he didn't deserve to die, but a lot of people were ready to kill him. Maybe he found the best way to end it all before somebody else did it for him."

"You cheated on him too," said Lisa. "It was never a happy marriage for either of you. Just convenient for you both to keep up appearances and keep the money flowing that you were both spending like it would never end."

"It was convenient for you too, Lisa. Bobbie always looked after you very well and he never cut you out of the will like he did me."

"What if there's nothing left for me in his will?"

"Maybe not, sweetheart ... but if there's nothing for you from his will, don't worry, you'll get something from me when it's all settled." Donna sat back with a self-satisfied smirk. "I'll do much better now. No divorce means I was still his wife when he died. Now I'll get more than he was ever going to give me. Pretty much everything, actually."

She looked pleased as she contemplated just how much she might now have all to herself, then she noticed the disgusted look from Lisa and turned her attention back to her. "You'll get some from his will, of course, but like I told you months ago, Lisa, I'll make sure you're all right when it's finally settled with your dad. Soon I'll know exactly what I've got to work with. Don't worry, dear."

Lisa did not look satisfied with that reassurance.

Donna continued, "Besides, I'll get a lot more from the insurance he had on his life. He wanted to cut me off as beneficiary and leave it all to you, but it was irrevocable, so he was stuck with it. Now that he's dead first, he loses, I win."

Lisa frowned. "Are you sure the insurance is still good if he committed suicide?"

"Yes, that's not an issue after all these years. He wanted

to stop paying for it though, in the hope they'd cancel it, so I made sure the premiums were paid myself." She sat back hugging herself and looking very pleased with her newly improved financial circumstances.

"Let me explain how it all works," she said. "We had a pre-nuptial agreement that meant we went into the marriage *common as to property*." She did air-quotes to capture the legal language. "So we each retained ownership of what we had before the marriage and anything we acquired after that was fifty-fifty, whatever happened. Death or divorce was supposed to be the same, but Bobbie was refusing to respect that arrangement. Now that I'm his widow, not his ex-wife, I'll get it all."

She tilted her head at Lisa, waiting for her to look as contented as she was with that happy conclusion. Lisa scowled at her empty coffee cup and said, "It all works out great for you, what about me?"

"Well, like I said, you'll get whatever's left to you in the will. But *la loi de la patrimoine* in Quebec (more air-quotes) protects the spouse first, regardless of what's in the will, so I expect I'll get all of his assets before anything goes to you."

Lisa looked up at her mother. "And all the insurance too? What's that worth?"

"The insurance is worth five million," said Donna.

Lisa was expressionless. Looking at her empty coffee cup, she said nothing.

"Do you want another coffee?" asked Donna.

Lisa looked up and stared past her mother with her eyes

focused on distant thoughts. "I need something stronger," she said. She paused. "You have any coke? I need a little sniff."

"Oh no, dear, you don't want that. That's a very bad habit, dangerous and illegal too. And there's no such thing as a little sniff."

"You seem to manage it." Lisa said. She sat back and glared at Donna. "I've learned all my bad habits from you, Mom."

Donna ignored the comment and said, "I've got a better idea." She stood up from the table. "I know this is all depressing and it's been hard on you, Lisa. Let me find something that helps." She left the kitchen and went quickly upstairs through the bedroom to the medicine cabinet in the bathroom. She came back with a small blue pill capsule that she set on the place mat in front of Lisa and then went to the sink to fill a glass with cold water. She set it down beside the pill. "Try that," she said. "You'll feel better. It's a safe, legal prescription, no side effects like cocaine. I have more if you need it." Lisa looked at the pill and left it on the place mat as she took a long drink of the cold water.

Donna said, "Don't worry sweetheart, we're both going to be all right. Now we can get on with our lives like you want."

7.

Later that morning at the office, Dale got an unwelcome phone call from Detective Claude Samson. "We have some more questions for you," he said. "We'd like you to come down to the station as soon as possible."

"Not today," said Dale. "I promised my wife I'd be home early for sure this time. Maybe tomorrow." They agreed to meet at one o'clock the next day.

Dale did get home early that evening. As he came up the front steps from the driveway, the door opened with Keira holding onto it and hopping backwards on one foot. Dale noticed her holding the other foot off the floor with her ankle tightly wrapped in white tape. He gripped her shoulders to hold her steady, leaned down to give her a kiss on the cheek, and stood back. "What happened to you, honey?"

"Didn't Mommy tell you?"

"No, I haven't had much chance to talk to her since yesterday morning."

"I scored the winner on a corner kick, a header right into the top corner! You'd have been proud of me, Daddy."

"I'm always proud of you, Keira. But what did you do to your ankle?"

"I kinda landed badly on it. I managed to limp off

the field, though. They called Mommy and she took me into the Children's for an X-ray. It's OK. Just a sprain, nothing broken."

"You don't have crutches to get around with?"

"Yeah, but they're too clumsy. It's easier to hop around."

Dale laughed and rubbed her head. "Be careful hopping around, sweetheart. You don't want to sprain the other ankle too."

Keira closed the door and reached up for her dad's shoulder to use him as a crutch as she hopped beside him into the house. "What kept you so late yesterday, Daddy? I could've told you all about it if you'd come home earlier."

"Well … I had kind of a bad day myself yesterday." He wasn't sure how to talk to his kids about a suicide. "We'll talk about it later." Keira was only eleven and Sean thirteen. Susan might be better at explaining it. She had more experience with death and dying from working with families at the palliative care centre. She volunteered there two days a week.

After dinner, the kids went upstairs to do some homework before bed, and Dale sat with Susan in the family room. He had poured two glasses of red wine and set them on the coffee table before he started to tell her more about Bobbie Brydon's suicide. Susan had never liked Bobbie, and his wife even less, based on the few times they had met at business and social events. After hearing more about the previous evening and the circumstances that made everyone suspicious of his death, she reminded Dale that she had never trusted Brydon and never understood why Dale had insisted on doing business with him.

"Why did you ever take him on as a partner?"

"He was never my partner. You know that," said Dale. "I picked up some of his product lines after his bankruptcy and asked him to help us with the suppliers and training on the products. He owed me a lot of money, so he was working it off. He and Lisa were trying to help introduce us to his old suppliers and some of his major customers. That was the plan."

"And how was he doing with that?"

"Not very well to tell the truth. He didn't accomplish much and now he's dead. Lisa was actually better at it then he was. She could be charming and persuasive, especially with the people who wanted nothing to do with Bobbie Brydon ever again. I doubt she'll want to come back to work for me now, though. I don't know what she's going to do. She was pretty dependent on her dad for money and a job, and he was paying her a lot more than she could make anywhere else. I really don't know what happens next for her. And I don't have all the answers for what happens next for the business either."

He reached for his wine glass and took a long, slow sip before putting it down again and sitting back on the sofa. "Sorry I missed you before you went to bed last night. I heard from Keira you had to pick her up from soccer at school and take her in for X-rays. Glad to hear it's only a sprain. She'll be running around again on the soccer field before the season's over I'm sure."

"Yes, she'll be alright. That's not the news I wanted to talk about, though."

"Oh, oh. Sean's in trouble again?"

"No, Sean's doing alright. Playing too much on your computer maybe, but he seems to be keeping his marks up. He stuffed your old Apple II under his bed, because your desktop computer is faster and it has a better screen for computer games, he tells me."

"Oh, boy. I hope he's not loading viruses onto my computer with diskettes from his friends at school. I really don't want to infect our computers at the office from this one at home. Our virus protection is not as good as it should be. I guess it's time I brought a new computer home for you and the kids. Not just for games. You can start using it too. We're into the nineties, Susan, it's time you got connected to the Internet and started using e-mail. Everybody's going to be doing it soon. The school has computers already, and the kids will have a chance to get ahead if they have one of their own at home."

Susan reached for her wine glass and said, "Fine." She took a sip and put the glass down before turning toward Dale. "We still haven't got to my news."

Dale looked concerned. "No? Tell me about it then."

Susan took a breath and puffed out before responding.

"You remember I went in for my annual mammogram last week?"

"Yes." He frowned. "Is there a problem?"

"Maybe. Doctor Brownstein called yesterday to say he wanted to see me about it."

"He didn't say why?"

"No, but that phone call is never good news. Something has him concerned, and he probably wants to check it out. He may want to do a biopsy." She swallowed hard to hold back her emotions and looked for his reaction.

Dale took a moment to get the word out of his head. *Biopsy.*

"So, you're going to see him soon?"

"Yes. He said it's not urgent, but I made an appointment to see him on Monday."

"That's almost a week from now."

"It was the earliest he had for me."

"All right, I'm coming with you."

"That's not necessary, Dale. He's only going to tell me what he found in the mammogram. He won't know what it is for sure yet, anyway. It may be nothing serious."

"Listen, Susan," Dale said as he reached to grip her hand. "If he's concerned about it, and you're obviously concerned about it, then I'm concerned about it. I want to hear what he has to say. I want to be with you right from the start. Whatever it is."

Susan exhaled slowly. She closed her eyes, nodded to Dale, and slumped back into the chair.

8.

Downtown near the city centre the next day at Montreal Police Station Number 21, Dale found himself seated in a dull grey interview room with a large, darkened plate-glass window in one wall. Across the table from him were the same two detectives, Claude Samson and Pat Carney. They had explained they were recording a video of the interview as it was easier than taking notes, and Dale had acknowledged his acceptance for the camera up in the corner of the room before they started. He also signed a copy of his witness statement describing the events on Monday evening that had been typed up for him.

He didn't notice Carney nod at Samson as he picked up the pen to sign it. Samson got quickly to the point. "Officers Cloutier and Dubé were right to call us in," he said. "Brydon's death was not a suicide."

"What? How can that be? We all saw that he'd shot himself," said Dale.

"What you saw was set up to make you think that," said Carney. He assumed a self-satisfied expression, like he had already solved the crime all by himself. He folded his arms across his chest and sat back, challenging Dale to try and test his assertion.

Samson spoke first and asked, "You knew Brydon was left-handed?"

"Yeah … he wrote left-handed." Dale frowned. "Played golf left-handed."

"You didn't notice the gunshot wound was at his right temple and the gun was lying below his right hand?"

Dale sat back in his chair. "You're right. It was."

Samson nodded. "Not natural for a left-handed guy to shoot himself with his right hand." He let that sink in, then said, "And there's more."

"What else?"

Samson paused and looked at Carney before he started to explain. "First of all, there was no suicide note. No indication anywhere from anybody that he might be thinking of taking his own life." He leaned forward with his elbows on the table.

"Then there's the gun. We cannot confirm it was his. It had the serial number removed and we have no gun ever registered to Robert Brydon. Where did it come from? More likely a gun used by somebody to commit his murder than for him to use it to commit suicide. We did find Brydon's fingerprints smudged on the handle, but none on the trigger. How'd he shoot himself without touching the trigger?"

Dale frowned again and looked from one detective to the other. Both were staring back at him and waiting for a response. "So, you think he was murdered?"

Both detectives nodded slowly. They watched Dale for a long moment before Carney spoke. "It looks to me like someone right-handed came up to him from behind while he was at his desk, pulled out the gun and shot him in the head. Then quickly wiped their prints and held Brydon's right hand to the gun forgetting he was left-handed and avoiding the trigger so he didn't fire a second shot and spoil the suicide scenario. Then he dropped the gun on the floor and rushed out, closing the office door before anybody arrived on the scene."

"That doesn't sound possible," said Dale. "How did a killer get in the locked building after hours and out again without anyone seeing him?"

Samson responded. "It must have been someone Brydon knew. Maybe he let him in. Maybe he was already in the building and just walked into Brydon's office. He didn't see the killer holding a gun and he caught him by surprise from behind. There were no signs of a struggle or Brydon defending himself."

"I see," said Dale. He rubbed his jaw. "It still doesn't sound feasible to me and seems like a lot of guess work by you guys. But if you're right, now we're back to figuring out who would want to kill him. You think it was somebody he knew? Maybe somebody sent a hit man."

"Not a stranger for sure, but not a professional hit either," said Carney. "Too clumsy a cover up with a fake suicide. Probably an amateur in a hurry with a grudge to settle."

He paused and leaned forward with his hands gripping the table to peer at Dale. "I'm guessing you've never done this before, eh Hunter?"

"What! You think *I* did it? Don't be ridiculous."

Dale threw up his hands and slumped back in his chair. "This is why you brought me here and recorded it all? You're accusing me of Brydon's murder?"

"As you like to say, it seems obvious," said Carney. "You were in the building, had motive and opportunity. You were heard yelling at Brydon earlier in the day. You could easily have gone into his office, closed the door behind you, gotten behind him to shoot him, then slipped out and closed the door again and gone back to your office. And you're right-handed."

He nodded at the signed papers in front of him and then sat back with his arms crossed over his chest. Again he had that self-satisfied expression on his face. *Case closed.*

Dale was shaking his head. "No, no, no. I never left my office all evening. Lisa must have told you that."

"Not really," said Samson. "She actually corroborated Carney's version. She was in her office with the door closed when she heard a bang. She didn't know for sure it was a gunshot. She opened her door and looked up and down the hallway and saw nothing. Her father's door was closed. She thought maybe something fell over in the warehouse or service department, so she went in that direction to find out. She couldn't get into the warehouse to turn on the lights and have a look because she didn't have the passcode, as you told us. Seeing nothing out of the ordinary in that direction, she went back and knocked on Brydon's door. When she got no reply and opened it, she found him dead at his desk."

Carney added, "Our investigator proved her handprints were the last ones on the warehouse and service department door handles. Her prints were also on Brydon's office outside doorhandle. But yours were there too, the last prints on the doorknob, both inside and outside."

"Yes, of course. I opened and closed the door, using the doorhandle. After we found him dead!"

Dale extended his arms, hands upraised. "Come on, you guys. You both know it wasn't me. No way in hell." He paused, shaking his head. "You can ask your boss, Hélène Bourassa. She's behind the glass, right?" He tipped his head toward the large window.

"You're the number one suspect," said Carney. "No one's going to make that go away for you. Not even your friend, Detective-Sergeant Bourassa. You need to take this seriously, Hunter. Listen to us. We need better answers from you."

They sat looking at each other without another word, until Samson said, "Gimme a minute." He stood up and left the room. Dale and Detective Carney had nothing to do but wait and stare at each other.

A few minutes later, the door opened, and Samson held it aside for Detective-Sergeant Hélène Bourassa to enter the room.

Dale stood. *Still too petite, young and pretty to be the boss of these hulking detectives.*

Carney stood and stepped back as she approached the table.

"Hello, Dale," said Hélène. "Claude is right, you do

need to take this seriously."

Not as friendly as Dale was expecting. No handshake across the table.

"We're going to let you go for today, though. I think that's all we need for now. But we still have more questions to be answered about the death of Bobby Brydon. We'll let you know if we want to speak to you again."

"OK, good. Thanks," said Dale.

He started for the door, then turned and said, "Have you told his wife or daughter yet that you think somebody killed him? Maybe it wasn't suicide?"

"No," said Hélène. "We haven't told anyone else that we're investigating it as a potential homicide. No one needs to know that yet. It may still turn out to be a suicide. We need to be able to prove it, one way or the other, before we make any statements outside this room. Don't say anything to anyone about what we've told you here today."

"Except for Susan," said Dale.

"Of course. I know you tell your wife everything." Hélène smiled. "Most of the time," she added. They both knew stories on that subject that they were not going to share with the two detectives standing beside them.

As he left Station 21 to go back to his office, Dale was thinking he should also speak to his friend, Frank, better known as Frank the Fixer, about the suspicions the police had that he might be involved in a murder. Dale and Frank had been through troubles together before and Frank knew how to keep a secret. He was also a versatile fixer who might be able to help Dale prove his innocence. He had been very creative and resourceful in the past when Dale was in a jam with the police and again when he was being threatened by the gangsters of Montreal.

Dale also knew that Frank was sleeping with Hélène Bourassa and they would probably be sharing this secret anyway. Dale went back to his car and mulled over the questions raised by the detectives about Brydon's suicide. Was he missing something?

He was driving up the Decarie expressway on his way back to the office in the fast lane, enjoying his sporty BMW-M3. It was a welcome relief for him to drive it hard through the traffic of Montreal whenever that was possible and he was not forced to weave cautiously through the constant traffic jams and construction detours and avoid the potholes that were so prevalent everywhere in the city. He knew his luxury sports car was an expensive personal indulgence and probably not appropriate to his current cash flow dilemma, but at least the sleek grey BMW wasn't quite as conspicuously ostentatious as Brydon's flashy red Porsche.

On the way up Decarie, he used the handsfree mic to call Frank from the car and set up a meeting for the next day at Dale's office. As he reached to tap the phone and end the call, he saw the car in the mirror behind him flash its headlights. Distracted by his thoughts and the phone call, Dale had slowed in the fast lane and the car was close to his rear bumper. Dale raised his hand to signal that he had received the unusually polite message from the agitated driver, then slammed the accelerator down and roared ahead to close the gap in front of him and turn his attention back to the traffic.

9.

The following morning, Dale was in his office at the small round conference table with his sales manager, Patrick Jensen. The table was bare except for their two coffee mugs set on small dark-blue leather place mats beside their open notepads.

Dale drummed his fingers on the table. "We need to get the sales numbers up, Patrick. At these low prices we'll never cover our monthly expenses unless we push a lot more product."

Patrick looked frustrated. "We're getting beat up on price, Dale, we're still not low enough compared to the competition. They must be even more desperate than we are to make sales."

"I know, it's tough. Everybody's sitting on high inventory they paid too much for as prices decline and the products go obsolete fast," Dale said. "Business sucks for everybody these days."

"We've got to bring in new products at competitive prices if you want us to get sales up," Patrick suggested. "The market is moving ahead of us and we need to catch up. We'll never grow revenues if we keep pushing nothing but low-price commodity products like monitors and video cards. That market is saturated, nobody needs more of the same thing. Now everybody's looking for the latest high-end technology products. That's what we need to have."

"I know," said Dale, "that's what I'm working on. Brydon and Lisa were helping us with introductions to the suppliers and some of the big customers for those products. We've got too many small independent retail customers selling low-cost desktop computers and they're failing fast. We have to accelerate our entry into new markets before we follow them into the ditch. We need to do business with the value-added resellers who know how to sell and install more sophisticated networks for the corporate buyers and institutions with big budgets. I'm working on that harder now that we don't have Bobbie and Lisa here to help."

Patrick grimaced at the thought of Brydon killing himself. "Yeah, it's a terrible thing Brydon did. Did you have any idea he was at that point? I feel really bad for Lisa finding him like that."

"It was a shock for everybody," said Dale. "And a terrible thing for his family to deal with. I don't think there's much we can do for them, but you might want to come to his funeral service and give your sympathies to Lisa personally. I'm sure she'd appreciate it. I'll give you the details from the announcement in the *Gazette* this morning, and maybe you can share it with some of the others here who worked with her."

"I'll do that. Good idea," said Patrick.

"Back to the sales issues," Dale continued, "we do need

to accelerate our efforts, but let's avoid giving anybody the impression we're desperate. Our sales reps and our customers need to have confidence we're supporting them with the right products and the right prices for this transition to the new world of high-performance computer networks. We need everyone to know we're going in a new direction; we're not going out of business. Forget about the home computer market and the low budget, price sensitive school boards and small businesses."

He looked at his notes, then closed the notepad and reached for his coffee. "I'll set up a meeting next week with Jean-Guy Brassard at Phoenix Systems. He has a lot of expertise with networking and high-end systems, and he knows the market well. He's willing to work with us on those products and he can introduce us to the best suppliers and some of the biggest resellers."

"Great," said Patrick. "I have a lot of respect for Phoenix and the way they do business. Jean-Guy can help us a lot more than Bobbie Brydon ever did."

"That's the plan," said Dale. He stood and took the notepad and coffee cup to his desk. "Thanks, Patrick, see you later." His thoughts turned to the other issues he needed to resolve in order to save his business.

Was more downsizing necessary? Now or not yet? Who should stay and who should go? Where else can I cut costs without doing permanent damage?

Meanwhile, I hope the cops don't start saying too much

about me being a murder suspect. Too many people are already worried about trusting me enough to do business with us, and the association with Brydon didn't help. Some of his bad reputation rubbed off on me, I'm sure. But I really don't need rumours out there I'm also a murderer!

10.

Frank arrived at Dale's office later in the afternoon. Marie greeted him at reception with a big smile. She knew him well and liked him a lot.

She knew that his real name was Faysal Mohamed Abou and that he had come to Montreal as a seventeen-year-old refugee from Somalia. The tough street kid had avoided the gangs and the drugs to fend for himself and stay out of trouble, most of the time going solo and working both sides of the street. As a young man, he became known as Frank the Fixer, with a reputation for doing whatever he needed to do to fix problems and end conflicts, whether he was looking after the Mafia and their friends who wanted to remain out of sight, or assisting the police who were sometimes constrained by their limited legal authority and had to play by the rules. Frank could be more creative and he played by his own rules. He'd rescued Dale a few times from encounters with the Montreal Mafia when the police couldn't protect him well enough. After years of working rogue, Frank had recently gone legitimate and become a licenced private investigator.

In the past, Dale had also called on him to help with some business issues that couldn't be handled by standard operating procedures. He too sometimes needed more creativity and a little stretching of the rules. He rationalized that all was fair in the viciously competitive battles of the computer business, as long as he didn't go to jail for it. His arrangements with Frank the Fixer had developed into a solid friendship between two men with very different backgrounds—the immigrant kid from Somalia and the Rocky Mountain boy from BC—helping each other survive the hard knocks of life in Montreal.

"Hi, Frank," said Marie. "He's in his office, expecting you, I assume."

"He is? I was just stopping by to say hello to you, Marie. I see you're looking good as usual. Keeping Dale in line, I hope."

Marie gave him a sceptical smile. She was twenty-five years older than Frank and never the most attractive woman in the room, but she did appreciate the compliment.

"I'm doing my best," she said. "Trying to take care of myself, Dale, and everybody else here. I seem to be the designated den mother, and keeping them in line most of the time." She hesitated, and then looked serious. "We had a very unpleasant incident here the other evening, though. I'm sure Dale will tell you all about it. Can I bring you a coffee? Dale's due for another one about now, too, I think."

"Thanks, Marie, that'd be good." Frank headed toward Dale's office and Marie went down the hall to the left toward the kitchen and coffee machine. She knew how they both liked their coffee—hot, strong, and black. She shivered with a little smile to herself thinking that would also describe Frank pretty well.

After the recent staff reductions, Marie was doing double duty as office manager and receptionist. She didn't normally bring Dale his coffee; it had never been her habit or Dale's expectation. But Frank was worth the trouble. When she came in to place the two steaming cups of black coffee on Dale's small round conference table where both men were seated, Dale was explaining the *very unpleasant incident*—Brydon found dead by his daughter and the police investigating until late into the night. Dale waited until Marie had finished flirting with Frank and had left, before he got up to close the door. He went back to the small conference table and sat across from Frank to continue his commentary on Brydon's death.

"The real news came today when I visited the police station downtown," he said. "I learned they're now investigating it as a potential homicide. They think somebody killed Bobbie Brydon. They don't think he killed himself."

"What makes them think that?"

Dale told him their theory about Bobbie not leaving a suicide note, being left-handed, and shot on the right side. "There were with no signs of struggle, so he must have let somebody he knew get behind him with a gun to kill him and then slip away."

"I see," said Frank. "And I suppose they think it was you."

"Yeah. They've got it in their thick heads that I'm the first suspect with both motive and opportunity."

"So, did you do it?"

"Jesus, Frank, of course not. You know me better than that. We've been through a few dangerous times together up against violent criminals, including a few Mafia gangsters, but I never tried to kill anybody."

"I do remember you thinking about it, though. Maybe even asking me to do it for you."

Dale scowled and thought about it. "Maybe once when they were threatening my family." He added, "In self defence I might do it, but I never had any reason to kill Bobbie Brydon. He wasn't my best friend in any way, but he wasn't my worst enemy either. There are lots of other suspects out there who might want him dead, if he really didn't kill himself. That's what I need you to help me with, Frank. Find somebody more likely than me, so the cops can spend their time looking for whoever that might be, instead of wasting their time trying to prove that I did it."

"I get it," said Frank. "But I'm still wondering why you ever got into business with Brydon at all. Didn't we investigate him a few years back when you wanted to buy him out and save him from bankruptcy? We decided he was nothing but bad news. You wanted to buy his business and then decided that was a bad idea, I thought."

"Yeah, we did. We learned enough about him and his business to avoid that disaster. His business, called BIG Distribution, was already beyond saving, and he was also into a vicious divorce battle with his wife."

"I remember. Donna Brydon, right. She'd already thrown him out of the house and was on the prowl for her next sugar daddy when I met her in a bar downtown. Quite a party girl, but not my type. She was on a real revenge tour though, wrecking Brydon's reputation and screaming about his bad-boy habits everywhere she went, flaunting her own wild and wicked ways all over town."

"Yeah, she's pretty special," said Dale. "I'm thinking she's one of the first suspects you should look into. She's had a couple of years now battling with him over the divorce, and she's probably angry enough and crazy enough to kill him. You should start with her. Maybe give her a second chance and take her out for a little, uh … inside information."

"I don't think I want to get that close and personal with her. I'll see what I can learn from the sidelines. But I'm sure she's not the only likely suspect. Anybody else I should know about?"

"Actually, I have a long list of possible suspects for you. During the bankruptcy proceedings the lawyers and accountants produced a document that listed all the creditors in order of the amounts they were owed by BIG Distribution. You'll see 3D Computers a long way down the list for about three hundred grand. Some of these guys were very unhappy to settle and sign off for ten cents on the dollar. Most of the big companies took their lumps and walked away. They're used to the risks of bad debt, but some of the smaller guys took a bigger hit than they could handle and were still after Brydon to make it up to them. He was under a lot of pressure. Not many were willing to make a friendly deal like I did. Maybe somebody decided to punish him with a permanent solution."

Dale reached into the folder lying on the conference table and pulled out a thick legal document. "I've copied this notice to creditors for you. It has the full list. Let's take a look and I'll tell you which ones might be a little shady and inclined to get more unreasonable or aggressive in their demands. Threatening violence or committing murder? I don't know. That's for you to find out and maybe point the police in the right direction, instead of wasting their time on me."

"OK, let's have a look and I'll see what I can do."

"Oh, by the way," said Dale, "your girlfriend, Hélène, is leading the investigation into the potential homicide and even she's not convinced it wasn't me."

Frank raised his eyebrows, but didn't comment. He shrugged and started scanning the list.

After they spent time reviewing the list and making notes, Frank said, "I'll take care of this for you and let you know if I find anything interesting. I'll talk to you before I share it with Hélène. For now you can get back to business and stop worrying about it."

He pushed the paperwork aside and drained the last of his coffee. "How is business these days? You were complaining about the competition kicking your ass the last time we met."

"Yeah, they're still making my life difficult," said Dale. "I'm trying to turn the corner and get into some new products and more profitable parts of the business. We need to make some big changes though, and it isn't going to be quick or easy."

Frank had been part of the process in the past, investigating merger options other than BIG Distribution, and doing background checks on the business owners for Dale and his accountant. Even with Frank's input, Dale had not always been cautious enough. There was a lot of pressure to make deals to save his business. He got into one bad merger that had caused even more problems for him instead of being the solution. He had only recently terminated that relationship and removed the partner by buying him out. It had not helped his cash flow, but it had given him the freedom to take care of business by himself again.

Frank was familiar with that story but wondered about Dale's other business partners. He asked, "What about Sammy Wong in Boston? Is he still helping you out with the business there?"

"He's already gone," said Dale. "Sammy had enough problems to worry about in Taiwan with his manufacturing business. They're getting squeezed too. The big U.S. buyers are all moving their business to China where quality is improving and their costs are always much lower. Sammy doesn't have time to worry about Boston. He wrote off his investment in 3D - New England and I may have to do the same. I'm trying to sell it to my old partner, Don Leeman, for whatever I can get."

"He was your original partner in 3D Computers when you started here in Montreal?"

"Yeah. When I bought him out six years ago, he left the business in Ontario with his other partner and moved to Florida to expand on his distribution business there. He can merge New England into that business and maybe salvage enough to keep it going."

"What about the retail business? How are you doing with your investment in the Canacomp Super Store?"

"We did well for a while, but I think the end is in sight for them too. The big box stores are winning that war—Future Shop, Computerland, Business Depot, or *Bureau en gros,* as they call it in Quebec. Costco and Walmart will be the next ones taking all the business in low-cost computers. Price is all that matters to those customers and only the big guys have the buying power to win at that game. I was lucky enough to get most of my four hundred thousand investment back during the first couple of years. Alex Simpson is hanging on to his customers at Canacomp as best he can and trying to diversify into consumer electronics. That way he can offer more products for them to buy while they're in the store. I signed my shares back to him last year. I don't have time to worry about an investment in the retail business anymore."

Frank was absorbing all that background on an industry in transition and leaving small business owners behind. "Sounds like the end is in sight for you too, Dale. Maybe it's time to give up on 3D Computers and run for cover."

"Hell, no. I'm not giving up on 3D. This business is still worth three-and-a-half to five million and we're not going down, dammit."

Frank was nodding thoughtfully. "Maybe there's something else you should worry about while you're trying to save your business."

"Like what?"

"Like saving your life."

Dale suddenly looked more concerned. "What are you talking about?"

Frank continued. "Think about it. Maybe Brydon's death wasn't suicide, somebody sent a hit man to kill him. And maybe he's not the only one they're after. You have some of the same enemies for some of the same reasons. Some people who probably think you hurt their business while saving yours. Maybe they just want you out of the way. Maybe they set it up for you to take the fall for Bobbie's death. If that didn't work, maybe you're next. Or maybe you were the target all along and they got the wrong guy. Sent to kill the boss, they figured it was the older guy in the big corner office. An easy mistake to make. You're in a dangerous place, Dale. Some angry and violent people may think you're the problem."

"Goddammit, Frank. I've got enough to worry about without you taking off on some new nightmare scenarios. Nobody I know wants me dead. They want me to pay their bills. And they're better off if I'm alive and working hard to do that. So, let's just spend our time on proving that Brydon committed suicide, or if he was killed by somebody, that it wasn't me."

"OK, don't get excited. I'm just exploring all the possibilities that might come up." Frank shrugged and gave him a tight smile. "Your friends at Station 21 are probably doing the same. I'll let you know what I find out as soon as I have something new to report. I'll try to get back to you before the cops do. Hélène is not your friend or mine if we're on the wrong side of this."

Dale knew that. He was not counting on her being his friend. He was counting on her being a smart detective and coming up with the right answers to the confusing questions swirling around Bobbie Brydon's death.

11.

Dale was back at the office early the next morning again before anyone else was there. After eight he started to hear others coming in, and soon Marie stuck her head in the doorway. "Good morning, Dale, there's somebody here to see you already."

"I'm not expecting anybody. Who is it?"

Marie looked at the business card in her hand. "Robert Martinelli, a reporter for the *Montreal Gazette*."

"I'm not talking to any reporters. I've got no time for that."

"He says he's working on a story about Brydon's death and wants to talk to you to get the facts right before they put it in tomorrow morning's paper."

Shit. "OK. I know this guy, he's very persistent. Send him in. Don't offer him a coffee, we won't be long."

Robert was a crime reporter and Dale had met Martinelli two years ago when he was reporting for the *Gazette* on the Mafia who had blown up Dale's car in his driveway. Martinelli had a good relationship with the Montreal police, especially the Organised Crime Unit, and he had a reputation for managing the news articles to help and not hurt their investigations.

Marie showed him in and they renewed acquaintances before he sat in front of Dale's desk. Dale remained seated behind the desk and asked, "Are you still checking up on me for some reason? I don't have any news for you on our Mafia friends and I'm not doing business with them anymore. That story is over."

"Glad to hear you're not in trouble yourself this time, Dale. But I was looking at the police file on Bobbie Brydon's death and your name came up. It happened here in your offices, right?"

Dale frowned, sat back, and folded his arms across his chest. "Why are you interested in the death of Bobbie Brydon? There's no crime there, just a family tragedy."

Martinelli reached into the floppy brown leather case he had set on the floor beside his chair and pulled out a small spiral notebook with a pen clipped to the spine. He pulled out the pen, clicked on it and held it against the notebook on his thigh.

"Well, I stay pretty close to what's going on," he said, "especially if it's referred to the desk of Detective-Sergeant Hélène Bourassa. She get's everything that might be interesting to me. You're right, it appeared to be a suicide, but it was reported as a suspicious death because there were too many unanswered questions. Now they're investigating it as a possible homicide."

Shit, he does know too much.

Dale replied, "Still only suspicions, no solid proof either way, I thought."

"That's true, but I did a little digging myself. Your name got my interest, then I did a little more background on Bobbie Brydon, your associate. I notice you've carefully explained he was not your partner. So I have some questions for you. What was your relationship? What was he doing here?"

"I thought you only worked on organised crime cases, especially when the Montreal Mafia were involved. There's none of that here."

"Don't be so sure," said Martinelli. "Did you know his wife, Donna, was connected?"

"What?" Dale sat back in his chair.

"You've heard of Giuseppe Luciano, known as Lucky Joey Luciano? Big time Mafia boss, he's been in the Montreal crime stories for about twenty years. Donna Brydon is his niece."

"I didn't know that." Dale had some new ideas stirring in his head, which he quickly shutdown, and returned to the conversation with Martinelli. He reminded himself that whatever he said might appear in the paper the next day.

"That's interesting, but so what? You're not suggesting she and Bobbie were working with organised crime, are you?"

Martinelli shrugged and raised his eyebrows. "I'm still looking into it and the police are too, I'm sure. Their names haven't come up anywhere I've looked so far. Maybe it's just part of her history and she left the family business when she hooked up with Brydon. They were both well-known party animals in their twenties and got into the social columns a lot, but they seem to have stayed out of trouble as far as

I can tell. No organised crime activity for either of them that the police are aware of either, apparently.

"The Luciano family is still in business though. The most active member now is Donna Brydon's cousin Tony, Lucky Joey's son. He's got a lot of history, mostly with corruption in the construction business, but he's also been accused of some murders and Mafia hits against his enemies in the other families and the biker gangs, but never convicted. A nasty character. Nobody messes with him and gets away with it. Maybe Bobbie Brydon made that mistake."

Dale was digesting that news and wondering about some of the names on the creditors list he had given to Frank. He didn't know them all, but he did vaguely remember one or two seemed to be in the construction business.

"Maybe Bobbie owed Tony Luciano money," he said. "I remember when Bobbie first got into trouble and I offered to bail him out, he told me to fuck off. He said he had somebody else who could help him out with more money than I could ever come up with. Somebody with more money than God, he said."

"But killing him wouldn't get Tony Luciano his money back," said Martinelli. "There must be another explanation. Or maybe the Luciano connection has nothing to do with it. I need to be careful that I don't report rumours or speculation. Just the facts, ma'am, just the facts."

Dale smiled at the reference to an old TV show he remembered where the detective, Jack Webb, was always using that phrase when questioning a witness. His mind then went to the *Columbo* TV series where the questioning usually concluded with the detective asking, 'just one more question,' to nail the guilty party. Apparently, Martinelli used the same tactics in getting his stories for the newspapers.

Dale added, "I don't have any more facts for you, Robert, so you and the police are still speculating on all the possibilities. There's no crime story here. You can keep working on your mission to shutdown the Mafia, but I'm just going to keep my head down and try to stay out of their way."

Dale stood to shake Martinelli's hand and show him the door. "I've got to get back to work" he said. "Good luck with your reporting, but it sounds like you have more work to do too."

Martinelli remained seated and held his pen over his notebook. "What about my questions? I have a deadline to meet for tomorrow's article. You know I don't like to make up shit. I don't have to print everything I know, sometimes that helps the wrong people. But I don't want to hurt the wrong people either."

Dale put his hand on the door handle and turned back to Martinelli. He looked at the notepad and tried to compose a quotable quote. He said, "Mr. Brydon owned a company called BIG Distribution that recently went bankrupt. His company was a customer of mine, and he owed me about three hundred thousand dollars which was mostly written off. Other suppliers of BIG Distribution were owed a lot more. Also mostly written off. The settlement in bankruptcy paid out less than ten cents on the dollar. After his office was closed, Brydon needed a place to work and try to do better for those creditors and help us all recover some of our losses. I gave him some office space."

"Were you getting preferential treatment as a creditor in the bankruptcy?"

"Of course not."

Dale opened his office door and waited for Martinelli to pick up his briefcase and put away the notebook. He shook Dale's hand and said thank you as he went out. Dale nodded at him and said, "That's the whole truth and nothing but the truth. Don't come back for more because that's all I've got for you."

Robert Martinelli looked back with a tight smile, tilted his head, and shrugged. *No promises.*

12.

Friday evening, Frank the Fixer sat at the bar in the Hotel de la Montagne and swirled his Rickard's Red in a tall pint glass. The classic dark wood and polished brass décor gave the hotel an elegant, sophisticated ambiance without being too posh or snobbish. It was designed to appeal to a mature crowd who liked to hang out in the bar and at the intimate isolated tables and booths in the dining room. It was not a place for young singles to party on into the night—no boom-boom disco music, no karaoke, no open-mic night. The Hotel de la Montagne was a popular place for older swinging singles to hook up—pairs of ladies and gents arriving together and leaving with different ladies and gents. Occasionally, there were single girls at the bar that a guy might have to pay for, but they were conveniently available for those who weren't doing well otherwise or were too impatient to keep working on their uncouth and unpersuasive pickup routines.

Frank was keeping an eye on Donna Brydon sitting with a boyfriend at a small table beside a marble pillar off to one side of the room. The boyfriend was overdoing the charm offensive — holding her hand and stroking her arm as she fluttered her eyelids at him over the rim of her wine glass. Frank had learned a few days earlier that Donna still frequented this bar. "Fairly often, not always with the same guy," said the bartender. "Usually a Friday or Saturday night."

Frank left his beer on the bar and went over to their table.

"Hello, Donna," he said, acknowledging the boyfriend, then ignoring him. "Sorry to interrupt, but I heard about your husband and wanted to come over and give you my sympathies. Very sad for you and your family." He reached for her hand and Donna set her glass down and held it out. Frank took it gently in both hands and said, "Please, take care of yourself. Have a good evening." He nodded to them both and went back to the bar without looking back.

Frank lingered at the bar chatting to the bartender and a little later noticed that Donna was leaving with the boyfriend. He kept them in his peripheral vision to watch their exit. Donna stopped at the door and left the boyfriend there with a gesture that meant, wait a moment, I'll be right back.

She took confident strides in high heels over to Frank with a provocative sway of hips in a tightly wrapped skirt. "Sorry," she said, "I didn't recognize you at first. We met here a couple of years ago, I think. It's Frank, right?"

"Yeah, that's right."

"How do you happen to know about my ex?"

"I've been working with a guy by the name of Dale Hunter and he told me it happened in his office."

"Yeah, I know Hunter. Listen, I'm leaving here now. This guy is too good in bed to go home alone, but maybe I'll see you here tomorrow night. We can chat about something other than my stupid fucking ex killing himself."

Frank agreed to be there about the same time the next night.

On their next meeting at the Hotel de la Montagne, Frank learned more from Donna about her and her dead husband, Bobbie Brydon. And he didn't have to sleep with her. He planned to share what he knew with both Dale and Hélène and get an update on what they had learned in the meantime themselves. Sharing information helped everybody to avoid erroneous conclusions. There were still a lot of unanswered questions.

13.

The next morning was Saturday and the weekend papers had been delivered. Dale sat at the kitchen table preoccupied with the business news in the *Financial Post* that was folded back beside his coffee cup. The coffee was getting cold. He had already browsed the *Gazette* and had pushed it across to Susan who was reading it attentively.

She got his attention when he heard, "Dale, you're in the news again."

He looked up. "What do you mean? I didn't see anything."

She handed it to him, folded back to the City News section, page A8, and a small article at the bottom of the page titled, "Suspicious Death May Not Be a Suicide," over the byline of Robert Martinelli, crime reporter. Dale took it and read the article.

"It doesn't mention my name," he said.

"No, but we know you're the 'business associate' who spoke to the reporter. It says Brydon was found in the office of a computer company located on the TransCanada in the West Island. It also says the police are still investigating because the suicide may have been a murder. Apparently, Brydon may have had some association with the Mafia." She frowned at Dale. "What's that all about?"

"Yeah, I'm not happy to see that in the paper. That's

Martinelli stirring up shit again to poke the Mafia. That's just what he does."

He reached for his cup and took a small sip of cold coffee before getting up for a second cup, then coming back to the kitchen table to take another slow sip and inhale the warm moist aroma coming off freshly brewed coffee. He set the cup down and tapped one finger on the article as he reread it.

"Maybe the police put him up to it. Sometimes they want to see what happens if they rattle the cage a little in public. Martinelli did come to the office yesterday to talk to me about Brydon's death. I didn't tell him anything he didn't already know and I didn't confirm anything about the suspected homicide. Hélène was quite specific about keeping that under wraps. Martinelli told me about the Mafia connection with Brydon though. Apparently, he *married into the mob,* as they say in the movies. His wife, Donna, whom you already dislike, is the niece of Lucky Joey Luciano and her cousin is Tony Luciano, Lucky Joey's son. You've probably read about them both in the news. Tony Luciano has been called to appear before the anti-corruption commission many times and has also been investigated in the several murders over the years."

Susan was shaking her head slowly. "It sounds like Brydon's death may be more complicated than you thought."

"Yeah. Suicide seemed to be the easy and obvious answer. But it may not be that simple. The list of possibilities is getting longer."

He handed the newspaper back to Susan. "I may no longer be the prime suspect, but they're not going to let me off the hook yet either. Meanwhile, I have to get some work done this morning. The other issues are not going away."

He got up and poured the remains of his coffee into the sink, rinsed the coffee cup, and put it in the dishwasher. "Life goes on, Susan, just a few more complications." He looked back at her unfolding the newspaper and opening it to the next section. "How are you doing with all this stuff going on? On top of your own concerns."

He came back to the table and reached out to squeeze her across the shoulders. "Are you ready for your appointment Monday with Doctor Brownstein? We still don't know what he found in your mammogram."

She stood up and hugged him with a quick kiss. "Yes, I'm fine. There's nothing I can do but wait, anyway. We have to assume it shows something. If he wants to do a biopsy that will take a couple of weeks before we know more."

"I have some meetings Monday morning, but I'll come home and pick you up to see him with you in the afternoon. Three o'clock, right?" Susan nodded. Dale said, "I just wish it didn't take so damn long to find out what it is he's worrying about."

"It isn't going to change anything. There's nothing we can do about it until we hear his diagnosis and recommendations for what to do next. I just want to be sure they get it right. Are you still going to the office this morning?"

"Yes, sorry. But it's always quiet on Saturday and it

gives me a chance to catch up on the paperwork. I'll be home by lunchtime."

"Good. The kids don't have any plans, so maybe we can have a quiet family weekend for a change. Maybe go out to a movie this evening. We could try the movie, *Cool Runnings*. It's about the 1988 Winter Olympics and the surprising appearance of a bobsled team from Jamaica. It's supposed to be an amusing and inspiring story of the underdogs doing better than anyone expected. It should appeal to you and the kids, sports fans that you are."

Dale gave her another hug and a hard kiss. "Sounds good. See you in a bit. It'll be good for both of us to spend some time with the kids and forget about everything else that's going on for a while."

Susan nodded and rocked slowly in her chair as Dale turned and headed out the front door.

14.

Early Monday morning, Dale sat in the luxuriously furnished office of Jean-Guy Brassard at Phoenix Systems, waiting for him to get off the phone. The classy décor was definitely a step up from Dale's low budget offices at 3D Computers and it made the move up-market to high-end computer products even more appealing. Jean-Guy also looked very corporate in a grey pinstripe vest and crisp white shirt with blue silk tie. His suit jacket was on a hanger at the door. Dale was still going with the smart-casual look of the 1980s — blue button-down shirt, no tie, khaki slacks and brown leather loafers.

Jean-Guy ended the call and greeted Dale with a handshake before sitting comfortably cross-legged in the plush leather armchair beside his desk with Dale on the small sofa facing him. Jean-Guy shared his condolences for the death of Bobbie Brydon, but he had been among many in the industry in Montreal who had warned Dale about him being crooked and untrustworthy, so he didn't show sincere concern for his unhappy ending. It would have been cruel of him to say *good riddance*, but Dale knew that was what he was thinking. They quickly moved on to other subjects.

"I think you already know which products I like for your distribution product lines," said Jean-Guy. "You have some good products that should continue to do well, but you need to add more in data storage and networking. The growth now will come from those markets. Your newest high-resolution flat-screen monitors will do well, and I know you have the video cards to go with them. High performance graphics are not so important to the corporate market, that's more for the gamers, but the serious buyers do want quality and reliability in all their computer equipment. Businesses all depend on technology now. Their computer systems are mission critical, as they call it, especially when they're seeking budget approvals for new equipment. We need to be conspicuous as the best suppliers in the market when they're ready to buy."

"I agree," said Dale, "and I appreciate your advice on what's going to work for us going forward. You've been a model customer for us and we respect that. You'll always get our best prices and terms and I'll count on you to let us know if we're still not competitive enough."

"Of course,' said Jean-Guy. "*C'est compris.* We understand each other." He smiled and leaned back. "We've done enough business together to know we can trust each other to be fair and honest, Dale. No contracts required. It'll be good for both of us to share information and keep referring business to each other."

"Great," said Dale. "I'm loving the concept already." He reached forward for a friendly fist bump with Jean-Guy, then leaned back looking confident and relaxed. "Now for the next step, negotiating contracts. I'd like your input on the suppliers I'm talking to. They all have good product lines for us, but which ones can I rely on as business partners? That's the key for me." He reached into his briefcase to pull out a folder which he handed to Jean-Guy. "Here's my current short list of potential suppliers after review with my sales and service managers."

"OK, let's have a look." Jean-Guy got up and went to the large oval conference table beside the windows where he laid down the folder, then went back to his desk for his empty coffee cup. Dale's was on the coffee table in front of the sofa. Jean-Guy added, "First, let's get a couple of fresh cups." He opened his office door and led Dale down the hall to the coffee machine. Back at the conference table, they spent a good hour-and-a-half reviewing the potential new suppliers and discussing the strategy and tactics for negotiating favourable distribution agreements. Dale left with a lot to think about, but he had a much clearer sense of direction on where he was taking his business.

In the car on the way to his next meeting, Dale was thanking his lucky stars for the good choice of customers, like Jean-Guy Brassard at Phoenix Systems, who were smart, honest, and a pleasure to do business with. These were the friends he needed for the turnaround of his business. The next meeting would be another test of friendship.

He had been doing business with Rick Petrie, the manager at the *Banque Commerciale de Montreal* since he opened 3D Computer Products almost ten years ago. Starting with loans of fifty-thousand dollars, he was now up to $4.5 million on his line of credit. However, his current financial difficulties had strained his relationship with the bank. In fact, 3D was now in default by not meeting the loan requirements for security and debt ratios, and had frequently been over the credit limit during the last three months. Today was going to be a test for continuing bank support from Petrie.

Dale was reminded of the old adage of his former finance professor during his MBA at McGill. "Always make sure your bank is a welcome and willing partner in your business." Petrie was still welcome, but he was becoming less willing. The risks were shifting to the bank if it continued to finance the uncertain future of 3D Computer Products and Petrie was getting anxious about it. The bank was never comfortable with the increasing risk of business failure and a client potentially defaulting on their loans.

In Petrie's office, Dale tried to sound confident and optimistic. He gave a quick summary of the plans he had just settled with Jean-Guy Brassard to add high-margin, high-end product lines that were better aligned with the current demands of corporate and institutional buyers with big budgets. He explained how that would move 3D away from selling low-margin commodity products to high-risk retail customers.

Petrie was shaking his head. "I'm sorry, Dale. I know you always have a plan to do better, but we're not talking about the future anymore. We're talking about right now, this week. You've got to get your line of credit back down by Friday or I'm going to have to transfer the file to Special Accounts. They've put me on notice. Time's up."

"What does that mean?" Dale knew it was not good for him and his business if he ever lost the connection with Rick Petrie at the bank.

"It means your account is taken out of the branch and is no longer my responsibility. Special Accounts is essentially the collections department. They would give you notice that the loans are payable in full immediately. That's what a demand loan means. If you're in default we can demand payment in full."

"By Friday!?"

"No. I have until Friday to transfer the file. Then Special Accounts would give you two weeks, maybe thirty days, to pay it off. If you fail to do that, or don't manage to replace us with another lender by then, we'll install a monitor from the bank who would take over control of your receipts and start selling your assets to pay down the outstanding loans. He would have to sign off on every cheque you write. Your service fees would go up to fifteen hundred dollars a week, just for the pleasure of having our guy in your office monitoring all your transactions."

"Jesus, Rick. You might as well just shoot me."

Petrie looked discouraged and shook his head slowly. "You've got to do something this week, Dale. I can't cover for you any longer. You'll need to get it under $4.5 million by Friday and I'll need a proposal from you on how you'll get it back in line with the required ratios on receivables and inventory again over the next month. Then you'll have to continue to reduce the loans every month, based on an agreed schedule. That's the only way to avoid handing you over to Special Accounts. I know you don't want that because then you basically lose control of your business."

Dale clenched his jaw and gripped the arms of his chair to pull himself up from the position he had progressively slumped down into. He was thinking it sounded fucking impossible to avoid a disastrous ending for his business.

"That's a lot to accomplish in a few days," he said.

Petrie nodded and forced a tight smile. "Maybe I can help babysit you through the process for less than fifteen hundred a week."

Dale raised his eyebrows and tried to look encouraged. "That sounds like a better idea."

"My going rate for babysitting is $1.50 an hour, but it's negotiable."

Dale appreciated Petrie's attempt at relieving the tension, but he was mentally running through his financials to find a quick three hundred thousand he could pull in to get his line of credit back under the limit.

Then what? He didn't know.

Petrie turned serious and continued. "This is a real deadline, Dale. Not an idle threat. I don't do that. Never have, as you know. We've been through some tight stretches before, but this time it's been going on too long and seems to be getting worse. No up-ticks, just a steady decline in both your revenue and your profitability. You have to find a way to accelerate the turnaround or find a rescue plan quickly, … somehow."

"That's what I'm doing," said Dale. "Unfortunately, we've had an unexpected tragedy this week that's disrupted my plans a bit."

He explained to Petrie the circumstances of Bobbie Brydon's death at the office. He concluded by adding, "Sorry about the wise crack to just shoot me, but I guess Bobbie's death is in the back of my mind. Especially under the circumstances. He tried hard to turn his business around and failed. Beyond all the things we've just talked about, he did like many other business owners who are desperate to survive—he lied, he cheated, and he stole if he thought he could get away with it. In the end everybody lost. Then he killed himself. Not the happy ending I'm looking for."

"I'm sorry, Dale. That's not a good story to hear at any time. I know you'll do better than most at surviving with your integrity intact. Lying, cheating, and stealing doesn't usually help. It just ruins your reputation for any future comeback. I'm sure you'll come up with some more creative solutions. I'll do my best to fend off the special account vultures at head office. They've got bigger problems than you to worry about for now. Keep my babysitting rates in mind, though. I may be looking for a job soon too, if we screw this up."

Dale smiled. "Sorry, Rick, I don't need another job to worry about. You're on your own with the bank. I'm more focused on protecting jobs for the people on *my* payroll."

Petrie could see he was concerned and maybe less confident than he had appeared on arriving at the bank. "I know that's adding a lot of pressure, Dale. Staff cutbacks are never easy, and I know you take it personally." He paused to change subjects. "How about your own family? Susan and the kids getting through this all right?"

"Yeah, Susan has been a rock for me to lean on. Not the first time we've had business challenges to deal with, as you know."

Dale paused before continuing. Petrie was his banker, but he had also become a family friend. "Unfortunately, she's got some health issues that need attention. We've had a bit of a cancer scare and we're seeing her doctor later today. He's worried about her mammogram results and he probably wants to do a biopsy. That'll take another couple of weeks before we know what we're dealing with."

"Oh." Petrie hesitated and looked concerned. "I'm sorry to hear that, Dale. I hope it's not more for you to worry about. Good luck to you both. I hope it's not serious for Susan." He looked uncomfortable, trying to find more to say.

"Thanks, Rick, I'll mention it to Susan. We're trying not to worry about it, but it could be serious." Dale dropped his head to focus on the papers in front of him and re-arranged them neatly on the desk before slipping them back into the folder. He squinted and blinked to compose himself, then looked up at Petrie again.

"However, getting back to other issues, there is one more

thing you might be able to help me with." He explained that he was trying to dig into the list of creditors from Brydon's bankruptcy and learn more about some of the companies that he didn't know. He was wondering about the connection between Brydon's wife, Donna, and Tony Luciano in particular. "You have access to company data that I don't and I'm wondering if you can tell me more about who's behind these companies." He handed Petrie the creditors list with a few company names highlighted.

"I'll have a look," said Petrie. "If it helps relieve some of the pressure on you, I'll get on it today."

Dale agreed to come back with better news on his finances before Friday. "Don't panic, Rick. We don't need your guys at head office worrying about us. I'll look after it."

He left the bank with no idea how he was going to make that happen.

PART 2

FAMILY MATTERS

15.

After two long weeks of worried waiting for biopsy results, Dale and Susan had just come from visiting Doctor Brownstein at the clinic. They'd walked out the front doors of the West Island Medical Centre to the parking lot in silence, Dale gripping Susan's hand as he led her to his car. He opened the passenger door for her to get in, and they both slumped into the front seats, staring out the windshield.

After a few moments, Dale turned toward Susan. She sat belted-in with her hands in her lap, lost in thought, taking long slow breaths. "It was pretty much what we expected," he said. "It sounds like we caught it early and it can be stopped right away."

She didn't move or change her expression.

He reached for her hand and held it in both of his on the centre console. "What do you think?"

Susan took one more deep breath and kept her eyes on the Medical Centre across the parking lot in front of them. "It's a lot to think about. We still have more questions than answers." She paused. "I don't want to have radical surgery if it's not necessary. And I want to avoid chemo or radiation, if possible."

Dale said, "Let's do everything we can to stop it in it's tracks though, Susan. I know you're worried about a mastectomy or losing your hair and other side effects. But we need to keep you safe from it spreading. Those things are all temporary."

"Losing a breast is not temporary."

"Please do whatever it takes, Susan. I love you too much to take any risks with cancer. One breast or no breasts, I'll love you just the same. We need to keep you healthy for a long time. That's what's important."

Susan puffed out another long breath and looked across at Dale. "Let's go home," she said. "The kids will be there soon. We can talk later, but I need to talk to my mother and some friends who've been through this themselves. There's lots to think about before we make any big decisions." She folded her arms over her chest, squeezing her breasts tightly, and pushed back into the seat staring out the windshield again. "Like he said, we can start by removing the lump. Then see what we need to do, if anything, after that."

16.

The next day, Frank was back in Dale's office sitting by the conference table with another coffee in hand, his long legs in jeans stretched out in front of him. Dale pushed his chair back from the table and sat with one foot placed on his knee. "So you had a second date with Donna Brydon. Did she tell you about her Luciano family history?"

"She didn't have to," said Frank. "You learned about it from your reporter friend, Martinelli, but I was checking her background and curious about her not using her original family name. Most Quebec women keep using it, even after they're married. So, I looked up the records at city hall and discovered her full name, before she married Bobby Brydon, was Donna Luciano. She could have used Luciano if she wanted to, but I guess she didn't like the history or the reputation that goes with that name."

"Did you find out if she's involved in the family business?"

"I don't think so. Lots of bad behaviour as a wild child of the sixties, but nothing criminal that I found."

Dale thought about what he had seen of Donna and her not very affectionate relationship with Bobbie Brydon. Her outgoing, flamboyant behaviour had always seemed a little artificial to him, a little forced. Maybe she maintained the façade of bubbly party-girl to avoid revealing the real

Donna Brydon—nasty, self-centred, and vindictive. "She had the best motive to kill Bobbie if anybody did," he said. "It would end the battle over a divorce settlement, and she'd probably get what she wanted as his widow instead of his ex. But you know her better than me, do you think she could have done it?

"Hard to see her capable of killing him," said Frank. He stretched his back and laced his hands behind his head. He gazed at the ceiling to think about it. "But she could definitely call on her family to look after it for her. They're very capable of killing anybody they want. But killing Bobbie Brydon doesn't really make sense for them. They wouldn't be too keen on getting into a divorce dispute, it's not their concern, and probably not a good reason to put out a contract on him. Donna's life wasn't in danger. She didn't need protection from Bobbie and he wasn't interfering with the family business." He paused, then added, "As far as I know."

"Maybe they had their own reasons to go after him," said Dale. "I asked my bank manager, Rick Petrie, to look into some of those companies on the creditors list and you were right about Agile Construction. It's owned by the family and run by Tony Luciano. One other smaller company belongs to them too and they were owed a lot more than me when BIG Distribution went bankrupt. Both companies are on the handle-with-caution list at the bank because of their Mafia connections. The banks don't lend them money—they don't need it anyway—and they don't ask too many questions about all the cash coming and going, in spite of the laws requiring them to report on large cash transactions. They're a scary bunch and no bank manager wants his name to pop up on their radar for asking inappropriate questions."

Frank smiled. "Hard-ass cops are careful what they do with the Lucianos and the other Mafia families in Montreal. I'm sure the bankers are even more timid about poking into their affairs."

"Right, but they're also hard to say no to," said Dale. "As you know."

Frank shrugged. "Donna said something about Bobbie owing them lots of money. She claimed he was in deep shit with her family for taking their money and then losing it in the bankruptcy."

Dale nodded. "Yeah, I think he was probably laundering money for them for years. When I looked at his books, he didn't seem to ever be making much money but he was always churning lots of cash. Smelled like money-laundering to me. I added up the amounts due to the Luciano companies on the creditors list and it's well over two million dollars. That's a lot of money to lose in the wash. And not the right people to leave high and dry in a bankruptcy."

"But killing him isn't going to get them their money back," said Frank. "I can't see it justifying Brydon's murder. Even if the lovely and charming Donna Brydon asked them to do it."

"Lovely and charming, eh? You offer to look after her, Frank, now that she's single again?"

"Nope, not me. She already has a good list of interesting prospects. One guy she's anxious to hang onto for the sex and another one for his money in case the divorce didn't work out for her. She seems to think she'll do well now that Brydon is dead, suicide or murder doesn't seem to matter, so the sexy guy may be the winner."

"She was definitely keeping her options open," said Dale. "Actually, the boyfriends might also be worth taking a closer look at. We know Donna can be pretty persuasive and willing to use all her tools to get what she wants. If she couldn't persuade her cousin Tony, maybe she got some help from a boyfriend to solve all her problems. They might want to help her settle the score with Bobbie in exchange for whatever she might offer…who knows? What do you think?"

Frank frowned and thought about it for a moment. "It might be worth following up on," he said. "I'm sure the sexy guy would be happy to tell me some stories of the good times he's had with Donna. Maybe the rich guy will need a visit from Hélène to tell his side of the story. Neither one is likely to be the killer, but you never know where the connections might lead."

"They both have a vested interest in Bobbie Brydon's death," said Dale. "Donna doesn't have to fight for a divorce settlement anymore. Now she's a wealthy widow. She may not need the rich guy, but maybe he can be the new Bobbie, supporting her expensive habits while she gets to play with all the sexy guys who show up. Nothing but good news for Donna and the boyfriends."

Frank was nodding in quiet agreement.

Dale continued. "Not such good news for poor Lisa though, having to put up with Donna alone now. She'll never look after her daughter as well as Bobbie did. Lisa's kind of lost without him looking after her. I doubt if Donna is going to be very generous, even with all the money she now has to work with."

"You're right, she doesn't seem to worry about anybody but Donna. Always looking out for number one."

"What a sweetheart." Dale looked disgusted. "She's enough to kill the appeal of marriage for anybody."

"Yeah, I'm glad I never made that mistake. Hélène and I have a much better arrangement. Get together anytime we're in the mood for it and keep to ourselves otherwise. You've got just about the only happy marriage I've ever heard of Dale."

"Yeah, I got lucky on that score."

"That's for sure." He raised his hand to stop Dale from responding. "You don't need to remind me, I'm lucky to have Hélène too. We both need to remember to take good care of them."

He paused, then turned serious. "How's it going with Susan's breast cancer?"

"Well … she's going for surgery this week to have the lump removed. Then we'll know better what we're up against and the doctors can tell us if more treatment is required. Maybe it ends with the surgery." He shuddered involuntarily. "Anything else scares the hell out of us."

"Sounds rough," said Frank. "I told Hélène what you were going through, and she wishes you well too. She wants you to tell Susan that her mother had a lump removed about ten years ago and has been fine ever since. No more cancer and no more treatment required. Hopefully, it'll go well for Susan, too."

"Thanks, Frank. I hope so."

"Take care of your family, Dale. That's always more important than the business." Dale remained quiet with his thoughts.

Frank added, "Meanwhile, I'll look into the Luciano family and the boyfriends, and figure out their connections to Brydon. See if there's more there than meets the eye."

17.

Dale had arranged a meeting with his accountant and his lawyer to discuss his plans for avoiding disaster. The bank was back onside to maintain his financing, at least temporarily, but Dale had not yet turned the corner. The losses had declined, but profitability was not yet in sight. The decline in sales revenues had ended and the more profitable product lines were now being delivered to solid customers with strong credit ratings. That had allowed the bank to approve continued financing for 3D Computers, although the credit limit had been reduced to three-and-a-half million. There was more work to do before Dale could be assured that his business had a future. He wanted this meeting with his advisors for guidance on the financial and legal issues ahead of him.

They had arranged to meet in Morrie Steinberg's office located on the fifth floor of a modest office building at the back of the Cote Vertu shopping mall and commercial centre. Dale avoided the crowded parking lot in front of the mall and drove around to the back toward the open spaces in a corner far from the entrance. He hated the hazards of distracted and inattentive parking lot drivers bumping into his BMW and tried to keep far from the congested areas where the risks were highest. As he pulled into the space his mobile phone rang and he glanced at the Montreal number showing on the handset mounted on the centre console. He knew that the newer models of cellular phones had more features, including caller ID so he could see who was calling, and they were more portable, but he had invested over two thousand dollars in this one. It was installed in his car only a few years ago and he didn't see the need to have a bulky mobile phone in his pocket or his briefcase everywhere he went, the car was the only place it was useful anyway, in his opinion.

He picked it up and heard the voice of Detective-Sergeant Hélène Bourassa. "Dale, we need to see you again."

"Why? I thought you were satisfied I had nothing to do with Brydon's death."

"Well, we're not entirely satisfied. You're still considered a person of interest and a witness of sorts, but that's not what we want to talk about. It's about how you might help us with some of the other unanswered questions."

"I thought I answered all your questions."

"You did," said Hélène, "but Brydon's wife and daughter have not been so co-operative."

"Donna Brydon and Lisa aren't willing to answer your questions?"

"That's putting it mildly. With expletives deleted, they think we should just do our job and accept it was a suicide. We're still not convinced either way, but I think you could help us with a little more background on Brydon and his family. You know them better than we do, and you also have some knowledge of his business dealings. It would be helpful if you'd come in and see us. My office this time, not the interrogation room."

"Is the coffee any better in your office?"

"That could be arranged if it helps to persuade you."

Dale agreed to meet her downtown at Station 21 the next day after work. He didn't have much confidence in getting better coffee.

A few minutes after the call, he was installed with a good strong black cup of coffee in Morrie Steinberg's conference room. Dale, Morrie, and his lawyer, Paul Macrae, sat in high-backed, black leather chairs around the oblong conference table. Dale was in his usual button-down casual style; Morrie was in a fashionable pink shirt with a colourful yellow flowered tie, his brown suede sport jacket hanging over the back of a chair. Paul was looking lawyerly in a three-piece, dark-blue suit, jacket on and vest buttoned up.

"Glad to hear the bank has backed off and left you alone to get on with your plans, Dale," said Morrie. "I hope they give you enough time to get where you want to go."

"It hasn't been easy to get them to stay calm and let me carry on," said Dale. "I'm going to have to keep making progress before they lose their patience and threaten to call the loans again."

"Did they get you to sign personal guarantees this time?" asked Paul. "I know that was a shock when they discovered they didn't have them on the four-and-a-half-million and your loans were in default."

"You're right," said Dale. "Petrie told me it's the first

time he ever heard his V.P. drop an f-bomb. Apparently, he exploded and snarled, 'How the fuck did we let that happen!'" Dale smiled at the thought of that meeting for Petrie and added, "I got rid of the personal guarantees long ago, when I was in a better negotiating position and threatening to move my business to another bank." *They probably wish by now they'd let me go.*

"I've never been a fan of giving the bank personal guarantees on any loans I've had," he continued. "They always ask, though, as if it's proof that you're serious. And I always explain that if they want my house when things go bad, then I want their house if things go well. They never find that amusing, but it usually ends the conversation."

Morrie laughed. "Bankers have even less sense of humour than us accountants."

Dale chuckled. "Well, they may still have the last laugh. In order to keep my line of credit in place I had to put more cash into the business myself and the only place I could get it was to add a home equity loan to the mortgage on my house. Petrie had to be creative with my account to finesse that into the mix. Poor Susan, she had to put up with me persuading her it was necessary to save the business and get us back out of trouble."

"It helps to have friends stepping up when you need them," said Paul.

"I'm counting on all the friends I've got," said Dale, "including you guys. When times are tough, you really discover who your friends are. I've had a few surprises, and learned to appreciate a few that I never knew I had. Reminds me of what my old partner in 3D Computers used to say, 'What goes around, comes around.' Now I know what he was talking about."

"Jeez, you're going to bring a tear to my eye, Dale," said Morrie. He laughed again. "You told me your old buddy, Frank the Fixer, has also been helping you out with collections."

"Yeah, he's done a great job, accelerating the cash flow we needed from some slow customers who were trying to ignore us," said Dale. "Frank is hard to ignore."

Paul interjected, "Isn't he the guy who works for the Mafia?"

"Uh-h-h… you'll have to ask him," said Dale. "He works as a private investigator now and I don't ask too many questions about who's paying his exorbitant fees. I'm paying him a percentage of what he collects and that's costing me less than either of you guys charge for collections."

Morrie asked, "Does he put Frank the Fixer on his P.I. business card?"

"I thought he should," said Dale, "but he thought it sounded too much like a Mafia hit man for hire. He didn't want to advertise that, and he thought his own name, Faysal Mohamed Abou, would sound too much like an Islamic terrorist for hire, so he decided on Frank Abbott P.I. for his business cards."

"I hope he's not using Mafia tactics for collections," said Paul. "That could get you in more trouble with the law and I understand you don't need more of that. Morrie was telling me about the suspicious death of your partner, Bobbie Brydon. Are the police making any progress on getting that resolved?"

Dale looked sideways at Morrie and scowled. "Brydon was never my partner."

"Sorry," said Morrie. "Look, Paul reads the papers. He asked about it, so I told him about your history with Brydon and the police not being satisfied it was a suicide. You're the one who told me they even thought you might be a suspect."

"I don't think I'm a suspect anymore, but the police are not making much progress. I don't know more than what I read in the papers either." Dale wondered if he would learn more from Hélène when he met with her tomorrow. *Maybe I am still a suspect.*

"Now can we get back to my business issues," he said. "First, to answer your question, Paul, Frank is too smart to get caught doing anything illegal." *I hope. He is capable of the rough stuff, but he shouldn't need it. He can be pretty intimidating just by showing up.*

"I gave him some paperwork, including one of your collection letters, Paul. Thank you. He's collected a couple of hundred grand in a few weeks and helped me get rid of a few losers. I was able to close their accounts without big write-offs, so I'm happy with his help and not too worried about any complaints. What I'd like to know is what else I should be doing. How do I control this for a safe, soft landing instead of crashing in flames and losing everything?"

Paul looked concerned. "I hope he's not using my name on those letters," he said.

"Nope, Frank Abbott, P.I.," said Dale. "Your letter was too polite, anyway. We changed the wording a little and Frank delivered it in person. That seemed to work." He smiled at Paul's apparent discomfort with their tactics.

Morrie asked him, "Have you considered any more merger opportunities? Maybe you can make a deal to sell out and take away some cash. Not lose everything. What about Jim Annapoulis at ABJ? Have you talked to him again? You turned down his last offer a while ago, maybe you should grab it now." Morrie had worked with Dale on his earlier merger and acquisition plans and they had agreed to turn down the offer from Annapoulis. Now it would be more than acceptable.

Dale replied, "He's doing fine, he looked after himself pretty well. He merged his own distribution business with one of the big guys and he's still trying to put me out of business. I think his offer to buy 3D has gone down now though, probably to zilch. In fact, I'd probably have to pay him to haul it away and I'm never giving Annapoulis that satisfaction."

Paul pushed a file folder into a manila envelope with his firm's name on it and said to Dale, "You might want to consider filing for protection under the Creditors Act. I've put some background together for you to look at. Filing for protection from your creditors would give you time to finish reorganizing and refinancing, and you can hold onto your cash until you propose a final settlement to all the creditors that's been approved by the court. You remain in control, and nobody can push you for payment or force you into bankruptcy."

"That still sounds like a last resort," said Dale. "It means I'd basically wind up the business, salvage what I can, then run for cover. Right?"

Paul shrugged. "That's about right, without all the legal language. I think you should take a look at it." He slid the envelope across the table to Dale. "Then let me know if you think it might be a viable option for you and we can talk about it."

Dale continued, "That's what Brydon and a lot of other businesses in distress have done. Probably more of them are going to be doing the same. But it's pretty hard to come back from that and do business with any of those people again."

Dale was shaking his head and looking determined to manage for himself. "A lot of people would never forgive me for losing their money, costing them their jobs, maybe putting their families in financial difficulty. I'm looking for a way out of this with a minimum of damage to people's careers and finances." He looked across the table at Morrie and Paul. "Not to mention my own career and finances." All three of them were silent for a few moments as they reflected on Dale's situation and the options for finding a way out of it.

Morrie spoke first. "You seem to be making progress, Dale. If you can continue to count on your bank to cooperate and you're able to negotiate arrangements that work for everybody, I don't think you need to do anything more drastic like filing for protection from your creditors. You're keeping them all onside for now anyway."

"It's your call," said Paul. "But you're definitely on a shaky tightrope with a flimsy safety net. There's no room for slip ups. We'll remain on standby if that's what you want, though, ready to step up when you need us. If you need us. Just don't wait until it's too late for us to save you."

"That's right," said Morrie. "Call us anytime and we'll do what we can. But keep doing what you're doing. I think your prospects are improving."

Dale left them and went back out to his car. He had a lot on his mind and was preoccupied with his plans for the next steps back at the office. Suddenly, he stopped in his tracks halfway down the main road from the rear exit of Steinberg's office building. He looked up to scan the parking lot. *Where the hell is my car?*

18.

Back at Station 21 again, Dale was sitting in front of Hélène's desk in her office. Claude Samson was in the chair beside him leaning back into the corner and trying to assume the role of interested observer. It was a tight squeeze with two chairs in front of Hélène's large grey metal desk, pushed up against the wall with a computer on the corner and cables hanging down to a power bar tucked underneath it on the floor. Beside the desk along the other wall was a five-drawer matching grey filing cabinet, filling the space and leaving a narrow passage for Hélène to get to her chair. She managed to slip through that space every day, Claude would not have fit.

The door was closed behind the two men and the narrow window beside it gave Hélène a view of any passing traffic in the hallway. She had asked Samson to lower the blinds and close them to block the view of anyone looking in. Dale's visit was not meant for everyone to be aware of. After only a few minutes in the closed office it was feeling hot and stuffy, but maybe it was the conversation that was making Dale feel uncomfortable. The coffee was not better, and he had already complained about it.

"Tim Horton's? I'd be more impressed, and maybe more cooperative, if you'd arranged for a good café latté."

"Don't ask for too much, Dale," said Hélène. "Like

I told you on the phone, we need your help to get some more information on Brydon and his family."

"I'm not volunteering to work as your undercover agent," said Dale. "I've already got enough on my plate. And I think I agree with Lisa, why don't you just accept it was suicide? He's dead and he's not coming back. You don't have a case and you don't have any suspects to prove anything else." He leaned forward on the arms of his chair and glared from Hélène to Claude.

Samson frowned and looked surprised at Dale's aggressive tone.

Hélène responded. "I thought you would be interested in helping us solve this," she said. "I know you don't want to remain on our list of potential suspects and your cooperation will help us clear your name."

Dale scowled. "You really want to play that card?"

"I'm not leaning on you to do anything unreasonable, Dale. You and Lisa already have us rethinking the suicide versus murder. Maybe you're right. But we still have some questions to be answered in order to complete our investigation. And we still have some other potential suspects who may have wanted him dead, suicide or not." She paused, then added, "Starting with his wife, Donna Brydon."

"You think there's a connection to the Luciano family?"

"We don't know yet. That's not your problem though, leave them to us. We'd just like you to chat with Lisa and Mrs. Brydon. Unofficially of course, to see if they'll tell you anything we should know. They both refuse to speak to us anymore and we're not in a position to demand that they do."

"So, we're back to the undercover role for me, spying on Brydon's family."

"Don't overdo it. Just keep in touch with them as you normally would. You're a friend of the recently deceased, Bobbie Brydon, and you're still trying to be supportive for his grieving widow and daughter, right?" Dale didn't respond. "We can chat again in a week or two and see if you learn anything we should know about. It's in your best interest too. We all need some better answers."

"I can be supportive of Lisa," said Dale. "She's going to need help to get through this and back on her feet. She's a good kid and deserves better, but her mother not so much. She's a bitch by nature and has never been a friend of mine. I'm not sure she'll talk to me either." Dale paused and rubbed his chin. "But I do have some questions for her myself."

Samson nodded and looked pleased.

Hélène added, "Actually, we still have some more questions for you too, Dale." She reached for the file folder open on her desk and pulled out a document that she read from. "According to your statement, you've done business for years with Bobbie Brydon and his company, BIG Distribution, then you got burned in his bankruptcy with a lot of other people."

"Right, so what's your question?" Dale asked.

"We'd like to know more about how he did business and who he did business with."

"Like I told Claude already, he was a pretty selfish, greedy asshole. He didn't have a lot of friends in the business, and he took advantage of everybody—employees, customers and suppliers. Pissed off a lot of people. He did a lot of business under the table and ripped off the government too, churning cash, avoiding taxes. He seemed to be making a lot of money, but it was all a cover for laundering Mafia money, I think. I can't prove it, but maybe you can." Hélène exchanged a knowing look with Samson.

Dale said, "If you have the list of his creditors in the bankruptcy, you have a pretty good list of who he did business with. It's even sorted in order of how much they'd like to kill him."

"We're more interested in who might not be on that list," said Samson from beside him. He leaned forward and the front legs of his chair thumped back on the floor.

Dale looked from Samson to Hélène. "I think you should start with that list and dig a little deeper into a couple of companies in the construction business. They're near the top of the list."

Hélène's eyes shifted from Dale to Samson and back again. "We did notice that," she said. "We have those company names in some other files."

Dale added, "There is something else you should know. Back when I was talking to Bobbie about rescuing him from disaster, he told me he had better friends than me with a lot more money than me. More money than God, he said. You might want to look into where his financing was coming from."

Hélène nodded and glanced at Samson. "Thanks, Dale," she said. "You've been helpful. We'll be counting on you to keep in touch if there's anything else you think we should know."

Samson smiled to himself, got up, and squeezed behind Dale to open the door and let himself out. He leaned back into the office and said, "All right, let's get at it. We've all got work to do." And with an encouraging smile, "Good luck to you, Dale."

19.

After the chat with Hélène, Dale decided to visit Donna Brydon at the big house in Westmount later that week. The stone mansion was more impressive in daylight, but definitely not Dale's style. Was it Italian with all the stonework and ceramic tile or Olde English with its high gabled windows, white stuccoed panels and blue wooden shutters? It looked like they were in an ego-stroking contest with the other massive mansions set back on intricately landscaped properties along curving streets on the slopes of Westmount with glimpses through the trees over downtown skyscrapers and the city sprawling below across the island of Montreal to the south shore of the Saint Lawrence River.

Dale went up the steps, rang the doorbell, and waited at the front door. He hoped Donna would be in a better mood than the last time he had been here. He had phoned from the car while he was downtown to say he was in the neighbourhood and asked if he could come by for a few minutes. She hadn't sounded that enthusiastic, but was curious about why he would come calling.

She appeared at the door in a dark blue sweatshirt and skin-tight black yoga pants, with heavily caked-on makeup and eye liner, immaculately styled blond hair flared back off her neck. The sweatshirt had FCK Fashion printed in bold white letters across the front.

Is she on the way to the gym or just back from the gym? From what I hear from Frank she likes to keep in shape, but the gym is not her favourite way of working up a sweat. She looks ready for a date more than a workout.

Dale shook those ideas out of his head and greeted her. "I wanted to see you again and share my condolences, Donna. I haven't seen you since the night of Bobbie's death, more than three weeks ago now. I hope you're managing to wind-up his affairs all right, and I wanted to assure you in person that I'm ready to help if there's anything you need from me."

"Don't shit me, Dale. You're not really interested in helping me and you're as happy as I am he's dead."

"I wouldn't say that. We managed to work together when we had to. We had our issues to sort out, but he didn't deserve to die. I still have some questions about that, though, and so do other people, including the police."

"The police are fucking useless. Trying to make something out of nothing. He killed himself, end of story." She stood in the doorway, not stepping back to let him in. "You said *you* had some questions."

Dale looked her in the eye and she glared back.

"Just one big question. Did you do it?"

Donna jerked her head up, startled by his question.

"You fucking idiot. Of course, I didn't do it. Did *you* do it?"

"Nope, not me either. That wouldn't even make sense. He wasn't much use to me when he was alive, but he was certainly no use to me dead. It would make more sense for you. The divorce was taking too long and going nowhere. I know that."

"You've got that right, at least. His suicide *was* good for me. No need for a divorce settlement now. I get everything the law says he has to give me as his surviving spouse plus his insurance, which is a good chunk of change too."

"But a suicide is not usually good for insurance. They may have an out if it was suicide and refuse to pay the insurance."

"Not a problem. I checked."

"Before or after it happened?"

"Fuck off, Hunter. You really are a pain in the ass. Bobbie always thought you were too smart for your own good. It pissed him off. He thought you had to be crooked too, you just hid it better than most."

"Nope, not me. Too cautious to be crooked. But Bobbie was definitely crooked and he didn't hide it at all. Even bragged about it and screwed a lot of people in the process. Actually, I hear you have some good family connections in the crime business who might have helped him with the crooked stuff."

She scowled at that comment and hesitated before she replied, cautiously. "They got screwed too."

"So, the whole family would be better off if he's dead?"

"We're done here," she said. "Don't call on me again." She started to close the door.

Before turning away, Dale said, "One more thing

for you to think about, Donna. Be sure to get your story straight. The cops know it wasn't me, but I'm sure they'll want to talk to you next."

Donna yanked the door open wide and screamed at him, shaking her fist in his face. "It was suicide! He was weak—a coward, a useless, worn-out old fucker. He killed himself because he couldn't handle it anymore! Nobody had to kill him. Of course there was no suicide note! He wasn't capable of explaining himself ... ever ... about anything."

She stepped back inside and slammed the door hard. Dale heard the deadbolt snap shut.

That's twice she's slammed the door in my face. I guess we're never gonna be friends. It's OK, I wasn't counting on it.

20.

The next day, Dale was in a meeting at 3D Computer Products with his technical services manager, Guy Tremblay. They were standing together and looking over the product brochures and documentation that covered Guy's desk. His office was just beside the entrance to the service department, a large open area filled with service workbenches and the electronics equipment required for diagnostics and repair. Several technicians were working on disassembled products and others were on the phone talking to customers.

Dale stepped back and looked at Guy. "I think we agree these are the product lines we want to add," he said as his eyes roamed over the paperwork. He stepped back to close the office door and they sat down facing each other across the desk. Guy could see that Dale had another subject on his mind and the fatigue of managing hard times and making tough decisions showed in his tired eyes.

Dale focused and said, "We have to do more than change our product lines, Guy. We also have to re-align our tech support staff. We'll have to make some changes in your department. Which service techs are we going to keep and who has to go? Who will be able to support us best on these new products?"

"You think we have to let somebody go?" Guy slumped back into his chair. "*Je n'aime pas ça.*"

"I know you don't like it," said Dale, "neither do I. But our current expertise is primarily in display products— monitors and graphics cards—and it's not going to be enough anymore. Our sales on those products are declining and we'll need more expertise on storage and networking products to support the new product lines. Maybe some of our tech support guys can be trained by the suppliers, but we can't afford to carry anybody who's not able to contribute one hundred percent. I need you to help me decide who stays and who goes."

Guy shuffled in his chair and looked even more uncomfortable. Dale was waiting for him to reply when there was a quick knock at the door and Marie stuck her head into the office. She said, "Lisa's here, Dale. She says you told her she could come in to clean out her dad's office today."

"Yeah, I did. I'll be right there," said Dale. "Just give me another minute with Guy. Thanks, Marie"

He turned to Guy after Marie closed the door behind her. "Think about it. Look over the training and skills for each of your guys. Theresa Leblanc too, of course. We should try to keep our only female technician, she's really good with our customers. We'll talk later. Come down to my office in an hour or so. I don't think Lisa will be here that long."

Guy didn't even look up. He continued staring at the paperwork on his desk and gripping the back of his head with his fingers laced deep in his long hair like he was trying to squeeze out a better idea than having to replace any of his staff.

Dale left Guy's office and walked back to reception where Lisa was waiting. He greeted her with a gentle clasp of her hand in both of his and then led her back down the hall to Bobbie Brydon's old office. He unlocked it for her and stood back to let her in. "The police released it to us just about a week ago" he said. "The office you were using is unlocked too, if you want to clear out anything that you left there."

Lisa paused in the doorway and glanced down the hallway toward her old office. "I'll check before I leave," she said.

She looked around the office where Bobbie had died. It had been tidied up and cleaned after the police had released it. There were a few file folders and Bobbie's briefcase sitting neatly on the desk. For an instant, Dale and Lisa both looked surreptitiously at the chair pushed back under the desk and at the carpet below for any signs of blood left behind. Neither of them saw anything or said anything.

"Not much of his stuff here to take away," said Lisa.

"Take your time," said Dale. "Check the drawers and cabinets for anything else that might belong to your dad. The police have finished with it and they told me they returned everything except the gun they need to keep as evidence for their continuing investigation."

Lisa shuddered and stood still in the doorway.

"Do you want to sit down for a bit?" Dale asked. "I

know it's been a lot for you to deal with—especially the idea it maybe wasn't suicide."

Lisa jerked her head up and looked sharply at Dale. "It was suicide! The cops are useless. They don't know what they're talking about."

She stepped quickly inside and closed the door. She reached for a visitor chair in front of the desk and slumped into it, scowling at the floor. Dale reached for the other one and sat down to face her as she wrapped her arms around herself and tried to calm her tone.

"You knew him, Dale. He was really down with all the shit that was coming his way. It was all too much. I think he just couldn't take it anymore. You know what he was like. He could get angry and make rash decisions. Sometimes bad ones, but he hated to wait on other people to decide for him. Like he used to say, 'Stop talking about it, just fucking do it!' That was his way and I think he just decided the time had come to end it."

"Maybe," said Dale. "I never saw it coming, but he certainly had reason to look for a way out and end it himself. But the police are not convinced. They're still suspicious somebody killed him and tried to make it look like suicide."

"But they're just playing around with their crazy theories so they can make something out of nothing. They should have better things to do. Go solve a real murder. They don't have any proof my dad was murdered." She had been staring at the floor and suddenly looked up at Dale. "Do they?"

"Well, they have some theories like you said. They're

thinking they have some evidence it wasn't suicide. Things that make them suspicious, like there was no suicide note and being shot on the right side when he was left-handed."

"No! He was ambidextrous—he used both his hands!" Lisa threw her arms in the air then dropped her hands to her knees and leaned forward to take a deep breath. She straightened up and tilted her head back to look at the ceiling for a long moment before turning to Dale.

"I've heard all their stupid theories," she said. "No suicide note, come on! Can you picture my dad suddenly deciding to kill himself then taking a moment to compose a note full of apologies and explanations? He was impulsive and decisive. Typical businessman—don't ask permission, never apologize, never explain. Just make a damn decision and get on with it. That's how he operated, and that's what he taught me to do, too."

"All that's true," said Dale, "but some things still don't add up. What about the gun? Did you know he had one? It was never registered in his name and it had no serial number on it. It was an illegal, unregistered gun like the street gangs use. How did it end up being used in his death?"

Lisa was shaking her head and shrugged. She slumped back into the chair. "They'll just have to figure it out for themselves. They're never going to listen to me, or you. I just want a conclusion so we can all get on with our lives. We can't even get his estate settled and insurance paid until the cops sign off on it. We have to accept some of the questions will never be answered to everyone's satisfaction."

She wrapped her arms around herself and stared at the floor again. Then she abruptly stood up and looked at the briefcase and the files laid out on the desk. She took a deep breath and said, "Let me go through this stuff and sort it out. I'll check my office too and then come and see you before I leave and let you know what I'm taking away. I won't touch anything that doesn't belong to me or my dad."

"Sure, Lisa, take your time. Let me know if you need anything else. You know where the coffee is, so help yourself. I'll be in my office."

A while later, Dale was sitting with Guy Tremblay at the small conference table in his office. The door was closed. They both had their notepads and pens on the table beside them. No coffee cups.

Guy tapped a pen nervously on his notepad and said, "What about me, Dale? Are you worried maybe I can't handle the new product lines either? I'm going to have to learn more about storage and networking technology and train on these new products too."

"I'm not worried about you, Guy. I'm counting on you to help us turn the corner and get moving in a new direction. You're a quick learner and a good manager. That's what I need right now and you're a key player in the new plan. But I have to ask, is it what you want to do next? It isn't going to be easy. It's going to take a lot of hard work and long hours from all of us. And there will be some unpleasant decisions to make, like we talked about earlier.

Not everyone is going to fit in the new plans."

Guy replied, "Yes, I want to be part of it. I like the challenge, learning to adapt and change with the technology. *C'est la vie en informatique, c'est l'évolution vite.* Evolution comes fast in computers, that's what keeps it interesting."

"That's right. That's how evolution works, you have to adapt to survive and thrive. Especially in this business. There's no more room for the old distribution business. When we started, all we had to do was buy large quantities of the latest products at good prices and sell them in smaller quantities at higher prices to make money and keep the customers happy. It's not that easy anymore. We have to add more value. We need strong tech support staff to be part of that process."

Guy was nodding in agreement.

"I did look at all the technicians we have now," he said, "but I still don't know exactly what you're looking for. You mentioned Theresa, but what about the others? What's really important to you in deciding who will stay and who will go? They all have different personalities and skill sets. Some are better at diagnostics and repair, some are better at customer service. And that's not all I'm worrying about. What about their politics? I know you don't like my separatist sympathies and there may be a referendum on Quebec separation coming soon with this government. Maybe you don't want some of us around when that happens."

Dale grimaced and shook his head. "The politics are not

important to me unless it's affecting working relationships or performance on the job. I know it can be disruptive if there are strong differences of opinion among co-workers, but the workplace can also be the safest place to discuss the issues and maybe learn from each other. Discover we actually agree on more than we thought. I still think I can persuade you to change your mind before the next referendum."

He laughed. "I know it's not an easy question for you, there's too much emotion and history involved. We won't put the subject on today's agenda, but remember you could persuade me to vote in favour of pulling Quebec out of Canada, Guy, if you can just arrange to pull it all the way down to the Caribbean for some warm weather and good beaches in the sunshine. Otherwise, you'll never sell separation to most of us Anglo federalists here in Montreal."

Dale sat back. "Does that answer your question about my decision-making criteria? Politics have nothing to do with it. Performance on the job is all that matters."

"That's what I wanted to hear," said Guy with a slow smile. He added, "I like your idea of moving Quebec to the Caribbean though. Maybe we can annex one of the islands there and add it to Quebec territory. I'll look into it and let you know." He was looking a little more relaxed.

They were about to get back into the paperwork and their discussion on re-organisation when they were interrupted by a knock at the door. Lisa opened it and said, "Sorry, Dale, I know you're busy, but I'd like to talk to you again before I leave. It's important."

"Sure, Lisa, come on in. Guy and I can continue later."

Guy got up and offered his chair to Lisa as he picked up his notepad and pen and left Dale's office. Lisa nodded to him on the way out and closed the door behind him. She sat opposite Dale and hugged herself for a moment before speaking.

"I was thinking about what you were saying earlier," she said. Dale noticed her voice was breaking and she had tears in her eyes that she blinked out and wiped off her cheeks.

"You may be right. It's *possible* my dad didn't kill himself. You've got me wondering now too. And then I found this." She held out a business card and showed it to Dale. "I found it in Dad's briefcase." She handed it to him.

Dale looked at the name on it—Anthony Luciano, President, Agile Construction Company. "Look at the other side," said Lisa.

On the other side there was a hand-written note in ballpoint.

$2.3 million – Don't forget me.

"Uncle Tony gave me his card with that note on the back a couple of months ago. He was at the house with Mom when I was there for dinner. When I mentioned I was working here with Dad, he said, 'Give this to Bobbie next time you see him,' and wrote the note on the back. I'd forgotten about it and didn't know what it meant exactly. I found it tucked into Dad's briefcase when I was packing up his stuff."

Dale held the card, flipping it back and forth to look at both sides. Agile Construction was the name of one of the companies he had seen on the creditors list.

He looked up at Lisa. "What do you think it means?"

"I think it means Dad owed Uncle Tony over two million dollars." She exhaled a slow breath. "That's a lot of money. He's not a guy you want to owe that much money to. He might be willing to kill you for it."

Dale frowned and thought about the note from Tony Luciano. "Or you might decide to kill yourself as the only way out," he said.

21.

Frank had asked the bartender at the Hotel de la Montagne when he might catch up with Donna Brydon's boyfriend at the bar and he was now seated beside him. His name was Serge. He was a fit, tanned, well-groomed preening forty-five-year-old trying to look thirty-five and prowling for any woman in the room who might be good for a fling.

"Yeah, I remember you," he said to Frank. "Old friend of Donna's, eh?"

"We met a while ago. Never got too serious and it didn't last long. How's it working out for you?"

Serge nodded knowingly. "Too hot to handle, eh? She's fuckin' dangerous, man. A freakin' Olympic gymnast in bed. Helluva good workout. Sexiest fifty-year-old in the city."

"Actually, Serge, I wanted to talk to you about her dead husband, not about Donna."

Serge scowled. "Whadya mean? I never knew her husband."

"You probably heard that he killed himself, but the police actually think he was murdered. I'm wondering what you know about that, Serge. Did you have anything to do with it?"

Serge's friendly, self-confident attitude suddenly changed. He looked alarmed, his dark eyes scanned the room before peering at Frank.

He whispered, "*Tabarnac*, man! Watch what you say in here." Then he sat back, peering at Frank more closely. "Are you a fuckin' cop?"

"Nope, not me," said Frank. "But I know the cops are looking for who did it. I'm just trying to help a friend clear his name."

Serge tilted his head and looked confused.

"Not you," said Frank, "another friend. I'm talking to you to help the cops find the right guy. We think Donna asked somebody to do it for her."

"Oh-h-h, shit. This is bad," said Serge. "The woman is dangerous, like I said. And not just in bed." He paused to think about how much he should say. "She *did* talk to me about killing her husband. I never met the guy, but apparently, he's a real asshole and wasn't cooperating to give her a divorce." Serge was shaking his head slowly, collecting his memories. "She was looking for somebody to help with a *better solution* she called it."

He paused to exhale a long breath and reach for his beer. He took a slow sip and looking at Frank, he said, "I'm talkin' to you, man, and it's the truth. You're not gonna fuck me up now, are you?"

"Not if you're telling the truth," said Frank. "But you'll have to convince the police, not me."

"Listen, man, I'm not bullshitting you. She wanted me to do it. Or to arrange it. But no fuckin' way. I'm not a killer and I ain't got the money to pay for a hitman. She wasn't gonna give me the money for it. She didn't want any tracks leading back to her."

"Sounds like you were ready to do it, just negotiating terms."

"Hell no, I was never gonna do it."

He looked at Frank and winked. "But it was fun letting her try to persuade me. The sex got even better. She wanted me to know how good it would be if we got married and lived happily ever after. Hah! No fuckin' way. And she was lyin' anyway. She'd just point the finger right away at whoever she persuaded to do it to save her own skin." He was shaking his head as he reached for the beer again. "Eventually we stopped talking about it."

"I don't think you're finished talking about it," said Frank.

He signalled to the bartender to come over and asked him for a pen and a clean cocktail napkin. "You need to talk to this guy, Serge, before he comes looking to talk to you. Detective Claude Samson at Station 21, just down the street and around the corner on Sainte Catherine."

Serge looked at the note on the napkin and stuffed it in his pocket. He didn't look convinced. Frank interrupted his train of thought as Serge wrestled with the options and the potential consequences. "You should start recruiting for a new girlfriend who can replace Donna for the acrobatic sex you like. I think that fling is over for you."

He tipped his head toward the other customers at the bar, downed the rest of his beer, tapped his finger on the cocktail napkin and said, "Sooner is better than later, Serge. Don't forget," and he walked away.

22.

"This doesn't feel like the offices of another jealous boyfriend ready to kill for Donna Brydon," said Hélène quietly, leaning toward Claude Samson. "Are you sure Frank's new friend, Serge, suggested this is the guy we should talk to?"

Claud shrugged without reply. They were in the offices of B.J Richardson & Associates – Management Services, looking uncomfortable and out of place in the plush reception area. Claude thought he might never be able to pull himself up out of the deep soft armchair he was sitting in. He was just realizing that as the receptionist called out to them.

"Mr. Richardson will see you now. His office is the one with the large door at the end of hall." She pointed to her left, past the closed door marked, Conference Room East. Claude resisted looking back over his shoulder for Conference Room West. They entered the large sombre office of Mr. Richardson and he came around from behind his desk and gestured towards two more soft, plush armchairs beside a low coffee table. He took the matching armchair on the other side and crossed his long legs at the ankles, straightening the pant legs so the creases were aligned perfectly along his shins toward the shiny toes of his black brogues.

He raised his wiry eyebrows above his steel-rimmed

glasses closer to his neatly permed grey hairline and posed the question, "I presume you're not here to ask me to manage the police pension funds, so what brings you to my office?"

Claude sat back and scowled at him, determined not to show him the respect he was expecting. Hélène started the interview. She explained their involvement in the suspicious death of Bobbie Brydon and their interest in Mr. Richardson through his connection to both Mr. Brydon and his wife, Donna. She waited for him to react or at least acknowledge the facts presented. He remained calm and apparently disinterested. He looked at them both and waited for more.

Hélène decided to get straight to the point. "We understand that you were involved in an intimate relationship with Donna Brydon and we're asking if you may have been persuaded by her to arrange or otherwise assist her in murdering her husband."

Unfazed, he remained expressionless and replied in a clear deliberate tone, "We had and continue to have a casual, occasionally intimate, relationship. She was very distressed by her husband's intransigence in her petition for divorce and she asked for my advice and assistance in getting that matter resolved. She probably wanted to kill him at some point, but she never asked me to help her do it. That is ridiculous speculation on your part. Or did someone else put the idea in your head?"

Claude pulled himself upright gripping the arms of

the chair and leaned forward to insert himself into the conversation. "It seems obvious to us that you would have a vested interest in helping to solve her problem."

"Grasping at straws," harrumphed Richardson. "I had no motive. There was nothing in it for me to have Bobbie Brydon dead or divorced. I was not going to marry the woman. We have a friendly, business arrangement and that is not going to change. Also, to save you wasting more of your time, I was out of the country at the time Brydon died. We have offices in Europe and I was in Brussels and London the week that he died."

Hélène asked, "What business are you in exactly, Mr. Richardson?"

"We offer financial services to wealthy individuals— managing their money, reducing the taxes they pay, making sure it's parked in a safe place, that kind of thing." His blank expression hadn't changed.

Hélène had follow-up questions. "Do any of your clients make their money from criminal activities? Did you introduce Donna Brydon to any of those people to help solve her problems with Bobbie Brydon?"

"We don't ask our clients how they made their money. We just want to be sure they have enough to make it worth our while to manage it for them." Richardson retained his bland disinterest. "And I already answered your second question."

Hélène was not done. "What was the nature of your *business* relationship with Donna Brydon?"

Richardson squinted at them before replying. "You know she runs an escort service, right?" The simultaneous blank looks and lack of response from the two detectives answered his question. "Ah, yes, she's a very capable businesswoman," said Richardson. "She actually helps me with my clients, providing non-financial services, you might say."

He released a slight smirk. "We do like to take good care of our clients. Whatever they need."

Claude couldn't help himself. "Donna provides hookers for hire? She's running a cat house, a brothel?"

Richardson turned toward him. "Not your everyday, two-hundred-dollar-a-night prostitutes, my friend. These are very beautiful, sophisticated high-class ladies who are very selective about the gentlemen they choose to spend their time with. Donna provides discrete matchmaking services for them to meet wealthy, classy gentlemen with no guarantees of romance or a long-term relationship. The gentlemen pay two thousand to five thousand dollars for the pleasure of their company for one night, depending on their expectations. Donna pays the ladies half."

Hélène asked, "How does she keep them safe? It can be a dangerous business selling sexual services, regardless how much the guy pays."

"It helps that she mentions the Luciano connection and I do the same. It adds to the excitement for the clients, and they're more careful about how they treat the ladies. Nobody wants to have to explain any unfortunate incidents to Donna or her family. The girls are safe. Donna even had her daughter, Lisa, working for her at one point."

Hélène and Claude exchanged glances and kept their expressions blank.

"I think that's all for now, Mr. Richardson," said Hélène. "We'll let you know if we have any more questions. Thank you for your time." He rose from his armchair and returned to his desk without further acknowledging their presence or their departure.

23.

A few days later back in his office, Dale was looking across his desk at Frank leaning back in the armchair with his fingers laced behind his head. "What do you weigh these days, Frank?"

"About two-twenty. Why? You think I'm getting fat?"

"A little soft around the middle maybe."

"What?" Frank sat up straight and sucked in his belly. "You think I'm getting soft? You want to go a few rounds and see who's soft?"

"Relax, man, don't be so sensitive." Dale laughed. "I'm not looking for a fight. I was just worrying about you being too big for that little chair."

"I'm too big for any little chair." Frank shifted his hips from side to side and the chair creaked. "You're overdue to upgrade this cheap furniture, Dale. It's been here since you first started on a low budget years ago. I suppose you're gonna tell me times are tough and you can't afford to upgrade your furniture."

"Actually, it's just the opposite. If I'm going to move up market with the big boys in the corporate world, I'll have to do better than my low-rent furniture from IKEA. You may even see me in a suit and tie soon."

"Humph. That's not you."

"Yeah, it used to be, probably never again. It's been a

while since I lived in the corporate world. We're not there yet anyway, I've got a few more important things to do right now than upgrade my furniture and my wardrobe.

"However, we're making progress. The bank's onside again and the new customers are starting to make a difference. No more nickel-and-diming over a few hundred bucks. The corporate contracts tend to be a hundred thousand plus for the systems installer who buys the equipment from us. Usually over ten thousand per order at good profit margins."

Dale was showing some satisfaction. "We're starting to turn the sinking ship around and we're not bailing fast to stay afloat anymore."

"Glad to hear it," said Frank, "but before you get too comfortable with all that good news, let me share a little bad news with you."

"What? You're here to spoil my day?"

"Just trying to keep you out of trouble, my friend. It's a dangerous world out there and you need to be careful with what you're wandering into. I have a message for you from the Lucianos."

"Oh, yeah? I'm surprised they even know my name."

"Worse than that. They know you had a conversation with Donna Brydon and seem to have accused her of evil deeds and then shared those ideas with the police."

"That's not true. I didn't accuse her of anything. I just suggested she might want to get her story straight because the police were working on a theory that Bobbie didn't commit suicide, he might have been murdered, and she was next on the list of suspects."

"Well, they're not happy about you getting her and the Luciano family drawn into those questions about Brydon's death. You might want to be careful what you say, before you give the Lucianos any more to worry about. They think you're sticking your nose in where it doesn't belong. They want you to back off. Stay away from Donna Brydon and stop talking to the police and sending them on a wild goose chase looking for Bobbie Brydon's killer. Especially sending them after the Luciano family with their nosy questions."

"I'm not sending the police anywhere. They make their own decisions. I'm just trying to help them make good decisions." He peered at Frank. "Who are you talking to that's sending me that message?"

"I started the conversation with Tony Luciano's driver, Vinnie Mancuso. I know him from way back and I asked him to put me in touch with Tony. I explained I had some connections in the organized crime unit, and I had information Tony might be interested in. So Vinnie set up a meeting. He picked me up downtown and delivered me to Tony's office at his construction company and drove me back to my car afterwards."

"And what information did you have for Tony?"

"Well, I actually learned more from him than what I gave him. He already knew about me from Vinnie and some of the work I've done for the other families he knows well. I told him I wanted to introduce myself and let him know how I might be useful to him someday.

"For starters, to prove my credibility, I told him about Bobbie's suicide and how the police are investigating it as a possible murder, and they know about his wife's connection to the Luciano family. All that raised questions for them about his links to Bobby Brydon. He knew all that himself, of course, but he was surprised at how much I knew.

"Then when I mentioned you, he blew up. He'd heard your name from Donna as the troublemaker who was tying his family into Bobbie Brydon's death. I tried to calm him down. Told him I knew you pretty well and I didn't think you wanted to make trouble. I offered to talk to you and pass on his message for you to back off."

"So you're working for me to look into the Lucianos, and now you're also working for the Lucianos to look into me."

"Yeah. That's pretty much my standard *modus operandi*, as they say in the movies, working both sides to keep you all from killing each other."

"Great, thanks. I'm feeling safer already." Dale was shaking his head at this development. He really didn't want to hear about Tony Luciano knowing his name after Hélène had warned him to keep his distance.

"Anyway, you can tell him I got the message. Then you can get back to work helping me prove who did kill Bobbie. I'm still thinking Donna Brydon did it, maybe with Tony's help. She had too much to gain and nothing to lose from Bobbie's death, suicide or not. Maybe she arranged for Tony to look after it."

"There you go again. Dammit, Dale, you've got to stop thinking like that and don't ever say it out loud. These guys are serious when they tell you to butt out. They're not asking politely. You need to be careful."

"But think about it. Bobbie owes Luciano over two million and Donna gets probably more than that from his insurance and his estate. Maybe she agreed to pay him off with some of that money and then persuaded him to look after Bobbie to get it. You should ask Hélène to look into it."

"I'm sure she will, but she doesn't need to hear it from you. Let her do her job without your help, OK?"

"Sure. I've got enough to worry about without playing amateur detective. I'll let you know if I have any more questions or bright ideas and you can share them with Hélène. Meanwhile, I'm going back to my day job."

"Good. That's a much better place for you to spend your time. Anything I can help you with? Maybe work off some of the fat and avoid getting too soft by beating up on somebody for you. Squeeze some more cash out of your deadbeat customers."

"Thanks, Frank. I think we're good for now. Please don't beat up anybody for me. Maybe you can do it for Luciano now that you know each other so well. Apparently, he approves of those tactics more than I do."

"Jeez, Dale. Now you're getting all sensitive on me. You sound like a jealous girlfriend who caught me cheating on you."

Dale laughed. "OK, your work is done here. Go make

trouble for somebody else."

"Fine, Dale, but take care of yourself. You don't want to have Luciano delivering the message himself next time. Actually, maybe I can make a deal with him to leave you alone. You two should be working together anyway. He has lots of cash and you need cash. It should be easy to arrange something, then you can be friends instead of enemies."

"Hell, no. I don't ever want to be in debt to the Mob again. Those are *not* the friends I'm looking for. These guys may have killed Bobbie because he owed them money, remember? I've got enough to worry about without adding the Mafia to my problems."

"Don't worry. Tony told me it wasn't enough to kill Bobbie Brydon for and he's not that fucking stupid, to use his words. But I'll take that as a no thanks from you and won't suggest any more deal-making." Frank got up and shrugged a smile over his shoulder as he left Dale's office.

24.

The next morning Dale was back at Station 21 in Hélène's office with Claude Samson in a chair beside him. Dale sat back and looked from Hélène to Claude and back to Hélène again. "So, what do you make of that business card Lisa gave me?"

"Not much we didn't already know," said Samson. "Brydon owed the Lucianos a lot of money and they wanted it back."

"You think he was into money laundering for them?"

Hélène replied, "Probably. Brydon needed the cash to cover his own problems and his in-laws always have lots of cash to move around. Except Brydon failed to make sure they got their money back. It seems like he was stalling and they were squeezing."

"You think they had him killed for it? That doesn't get their money back does it?"

Samson answered, "Sometimes they just want to send a message. You pay or you die."

"Then why make it look like a suicide?" asked Dale.

"That's what doesn't make sense," said Hélène. "If they wanted to send a message it would be a public execution, not a fake suicide. And if they wanted it to look like a suicide they'd do a helluva lot better job of it than this. We still don't know anything for sure. Too many trails leading in different directions."

Dale rubbed his chin, looked at them both, and asked, "So maybe they arranged it, but didn't do it. Somebody else did a bad job of it. What about Donna Brydon? Do you think she might have done it? Or they asked her to do it and she hired an amateur?"

"Those are all possibilities," said Hélène. "We're still trying to fill in the blanks. It could be we're looking in all the wrong places. Maybe it has nothing to do with Brydon's wife or the Lucianos. You said a lot of other people might have reasons to kill him, Dale, so we need to keep looking into them too. And we might even have to conclude it was a suicide. Brydon did himself in, he just didn't do it very well."

"That's a long list of possibilities," said Dale. "Let's recap. Maybe Brydon killed himself as we all thought when we found him dead in the office. Maybe somebody he knew came in and killed him. Maybe his wife did it or arranged it. Maybe the Lucianos killed him for failing to pay what he owed them. Maybe somebody on the list of angry creditors decided to take revenge and one of them killed him or had him killed. It could be any one of those or any combination of some of those people. How the hell are you going to prove anything?"

"We don't have proof of anything yet,' said Hélène. "We're working on it."

Dale interjected, "If we're going to continue this, do you think we could improve on the coffee at least?" He held up the Styrofoam cup they had placed on the desk for him. "This stuff is going to ruin my day."

"Sorry you don't like our coffee," said Samson. "I'm sure you're one of those coffee snobs who insist on their over-priced Starbucks everyday. It kinda goes with your sporty BMW. There's a Starbucks a few blocks away, but you'll have to go get it and pay for it yourself. Maybe later."

"Actually, I prefer Second Cup," said Dale. "It's just as good as Starbucks, maybe a little cheaper, less status conscious and a great Canadian success story. Did you know the company was started by a delinquent young man living on the streets of Vancouver, kicked out of the house by his parents? He finally hit rock bottom and bounced up to start importing specialty coffee. He and his partner did well demonstrating how good the coffee was by giving away free samples. People loved the coffee so much, especially compared to our national obsession with Tim Horton's cheap and disgusting imitation coffee, that they started charging for the samples and created the first modern specialty coffee shop. Starbucks soon followed their lead and became an international success story with about twenty thousand coffee shops around the world, while Second Cup stayed at home in a few locations across the country—typical humble, unambitious Canadians."

"Fascinating story," said Hélène, shaking her head, "but can we get back to business, please? The humble police officers around here settle for our own disgusting imitation coffee, Dale, so you can too. You can pick up your preferred brand on the way back to the office. Let's finish this while we've got you here. We're not done yet."

"Let's start with a few things we do know," said Samson. "Lisa says she heard somebody with her dad and thought it was you, but we now think it was somebody else that Brydon knew and he let them into the building and then his office. Maybe that person was gone by the time Brydon killed himself, but I still think he was murdered. It was not suicide. There are a lot of people with motive. We just went through the list. We need to keep working the list until somebody gives us the clues we need to close this. If we can't find enough clear evidence, maybe we can squeeze a confession out of somebody."

A silence descended on the office as all three of them thought about the recap of possibilities and suspects and tried to decipher some new clues from what they already knew.

"I think you need to dig deeper into Bobbie's business finances," said Dale. "I know he was cooking the books and a lot of it didn't smell good. That's why I backed away and withdrew my offer to help him avoid bankruptcy. Let's not be distracted by what we know about the money laundering with the Lucianos. Maybe there was other Mafia money involved. Maybe another family was competing for Brydon's business. There are a few other anonymous numbered companies on that creditors list I gave you and a lot of other companies with unhappy owners and a grudge to settle. Bobbie pissed off a lot of people and managed to save himself at their expense. He didn't give a damn who got hurt in the process. He was determined to look after number one."

"He even managed to keep the Porsche," said Samson.

"Yeah, that didn't help," said Dale with a nod.

Samson said, "I'll arrange a little more research on that list, Hélène. I'll let you know if we come up with anything worth pursuing." He hefted himself up out of his chair and looked at Hélène to confirm the meeting was over.

"I think I need to have another chat with Lisa," said Hélène. "She might have the clue we're looking for. She just doesn't know it yet."

25.

Lisa asked, "Why would you ever want to be a cop in the first place?"

"I still ask myself that question sometimes," said Hélène. They were sitting opposite each other, Hélène on the sofa and Lisa in an armchair beside the windows of her small apartment. She lived in Lower Westmount, below the family mansion on the mountainside, in a modern apartment building just above Sherbrooke Street and only a few blocks from Hélène's office at Station 21. Hélène had called Lisa to request a personal and private meeting for an update on the investigation into her father's death. She had opened with an apology for upsetting her and her mother with the earlier questioning and then suggested they should try again. Just an informal chat, woman-to-woman, not a police interrogation. She had tried to be reassuring and persuasive and Lisa had eventually agreed it might be helpful to relieve the tension and answer some of the remaining questions they both still had.

Hélène arrived by taxi, no patrol car and no other detective, dressed in a dark blue jacket over a white blouse and matching blue skirt. Her gun holster and badge holder were pushed back on her belt out of sight under the jacket. She wore the look of a concerned older sister, not the accusing officer in a murder case. She was a good actor.

Lisa asked again, "So how do you explain it? It's hard enough for a woman to get ahead in any career. I imagine the police force must be worse than most."

"It was a challenge, for sure. I wanted to be a cop, though. I think it was because of the experience my brothers had in their encounters with the police when they were younger growing up on the Reserve. They had quite a few run-ins with a lot of them. They were both pretty rebellious and tangled with the Mohawk Police Force in Kahnawake, the QPP provincial police on the South Shore, and the Montreal police in the city. It made a big difference whether they met up with good cops or bad cops—some were racist, some were just incompetent bullies, and some really tried hard to get them on a better path. Away from all the issues they had with the drug trade and the street gangs." Her face clouded and her eyes lost their focus on Lisa as the memories momentarily came back to her.

She returned to Lisa's question. "I decided I could make a difference too, if I was one of the good cops."

"You mean aside from being a woman, you're also part Indian?"

"Yes," Hélène smiled. "Half-breeds they used to call us. Our family is actually a mix of Mohawk, French-Canadian, and Irish, which should be good for us to blend in with others born and raised in Quebec, but we look more Indian than anything else. That's all some people ever see." She flicked her long straight black hair off her shoulder and shrugged at Lisa.

"It's beautiful," said Lisa, pushing her blond curls behind her ear. "It sounds like you were up against a lot to get where you are now."

"Like you said, we have to learn how to get past the obstacles and not let anybody hold us back."

Lisa smiled. "I'm kind of a half-breed myself," she said. "Half-Jewish, half-Italian. Not sure what career path that means for me, though. My dad wanted me to work with him in the computer business and my mom just wanted me to enjoy life and fight for whatever I could get. Fight like a girl, of course. Dirty if necessary, but always be a lady. Look delicate and fragile, but be tough."

She paused to reflect on her parents' influences. "My dad told me the same, basically. Know how to take care of yourself. Get what you want, whatever it takes. You might lose a few friends along the way, but don't lose any sleep over it."

"Sounds like a way to stay alone, without any friends," said Hélène.

"Well, that's my parents. They've always been a challenge. Hard to manage and hard to live with. Not easy to follow their advice, either. Let's just say they made me what I am." She slumped back into her armchair and lowered her voice. "Not my dad anymore. Now it's just my mom."

Hélène put on her concerned big sister face again. "Their divorce battles must have been hard for you, Lisa, and now you have to deal with all this on top of it. How are you doing?"

"It hasn't been easy." She choked back a sob. "It was a shock to find my dad like that. To think he killed himself and I never even saw it coming. How could that happen?"

"It's hard," said Hélène. "Especially being the first to find him like that."

Lisa nodded and wrapped her arms around herself. She said quietly, "And then I had to tell my mom."

"How is she doing with all this?" asked Hélène.

Lisa looked up and said, "She didn't care about him anyway. She's quite happy about it, actually. My dad's death solved all her problems. No need to fight for a big divorce settlement. Now she does even better as his widow with a big insurance policy, apparently. And she doesn't give a damn about me. I'll probably get nothing from his will or his insurance. And I'm out of a job. Now she's just a bigger problem for me to manage without my dad to lean on."

Hélène nodded, before saying, "And we're making it even harder for you by investigating it as a suspicious death and asking a lot of difficult questions. I'm sorry about that, Lisa, but we have to do our job and satisfy everybody about what really happened to your dad. Are you still convinced that he committed suicide?"

Lisa sat upright and let out a long sigh. "I don't know any more. I found him dead with a gun on the floor beside him. You're telling me maybe it was a fake suicide. But who would do that? And why?"

"We still have the same questions ourselves. But like you just said, your mother was better off with him dead, maybe somebody else felt the same way."

Lisa frowned and slumped back into her chair with her arms wrapped around herself again. She looked up at Hélène. "You think maybe my mom did it?"

"Do you think she's capable?"

"I think she probably wanted to, but I don't think she could do it." She paused and thought a little longer. "But she could have arranged for somebody to do it."

"What do you mean?"

"Uncle Tony would do it for her. He knows what to do."

After leaving Lisa's apartment, Hélène, walked back down to Saint Catherine Street and turned right toward Station 21. She glanced at her watch and decided she didn't have time to go back to her office before meeting Frank for coffee. She continued on the sidewalk west past the police station, past the line-up into the street for the McDonald's restaurant, across *Rue Guy* at the traffic lights and past another crowd jammed into the entrance to Starbucks before turning into the Second Cup coffee shop and walking past the line-up at the counter to a table in the corner where Frank sat in front of two large cups of café latte, each with an intricate leaf pattern drawn into the white foam.

"Thanks for the coffee, Frank," said Hélène, taking her seat. "You'll have to explain to me what Dale Hunter finds so special about this place. The students from Concordia and everybody else seem to be happy with their choices at McDonald's and Starbucks."

"It's not just about the coffee for Dale," said Frank. "It's all about their story, their branding as he calls it, and being a loyal customer. It's what he works so hard at with his own company. You haven't heard his speech about how the product is always less important than the people and their story? How it's all about loyal customers buying from the people they like and the companies they respect?"

"Actually, I think he started on that speech with me and Claude and I had to cut him off, so thanks for the short version."

"I'm sure he'll find another chance. It's one of his favourite subjects, so you might have to cut him off again."

"I can always threaten to arrest him again. That gets him focused on what I'm interested in." She smiled and took a careful sip of coffee without destroying the pattern in the foam.

Frank was enjoying a sip of his coffee and worrying less about disturbing the foam. He glanced at the student at the next table who had strategically placed his notebook computer beside his writing pad and his coffee cup near the edge of the small round table and was tapping gently at the keyboard to avoid bumping anything onto the floor. Frank decided he was not paying attention to their conversation, as his concentration had not been interrupted at Hélène's use of the words *arrest him again*.

"I hope you've got better suspects than Dale by now," he said.

Hélène also glanced at the young man tapping at his

keyboard and leaned forward to speak softly. "Actually, I just had a good conversation with Lisa." She deliberately omitted reference to the last name. "She's given me even more good reasons to follow up with her mother and her Uncle Tony."

Frank raised his coffee cup to Hélène and said, "Good call. That's where I'd be looking too. Those two are probably already partners in crime and it would be easy to see them working together to commit a murder."

The young man at the next table suddenly looked up at them when he heard the word *murder*. A hard look from Frank sent him back to focus on his computer screen, his fingers now frozen in place on the keyboard. He gulped and slowly moved his hand to his coffee cup, lifting it to his lips, never taking his eyes off the computer.

Frank smiled and tipped his head to Hélène. "So, how do you like the coffee?"

"It is good," said Hélène. She relaxed back into her chair and took another sip. "I should probably come here more often to clear my head and get away from all the interruptions. It's a good place be alone with my thoughts and look for more *murderers*." She emphasized the word this time and tilted her head to the student staring at his computer screen.

His eyes widened and he swallowed slowly, glanced at his nearly empty coffee cup and closed his laptop before picking it up with his writing pad and stuffing them both into his backpack sitting on the floor beside his feet. He turned away from them, got up, pulled the backpack over his shoulder, and walked away with one quick glance back toward them as he went out the front door to the street and disappeared into the crowd.

"I have another thought for you," said Frank. Hélène was still looking out to the street and smiling at the thought of the young man having something new to talk about when he got to his next class. She turned to Frank and waited for him to continue.

"Maybe you're trying too hard to find a murderer when it really was a suicide," he said.

"I thought you just agreed we had two likely suspects in Donna Brydon and Tony Luciano."

"That's it," said Frank, "there are too many likely suspects. A lot of people wanted him dead and might have benefitted from his death. But maybe he did kill himself. It is possible and also easy to believe. Maybe hard to prove, but he definitely had good reasons to do it. His situation was hopeless, with pressure from his family and his business associates to fix things he couldn't fix. Suicide was the easy way to fix everything. Maybe the only way."

"I agree," said Hélène. "It's still a possible explanation for his death, but I can't prove it either way. The only way it ends for me is to chase down all the suspects until I can eliminate them all as potential killers. Then we'll have to accept it was suicide. Maybe. It's possible, but probable? I still need to be convinced. Not finding the murderer doesn't mean he wasn't murdered. It just means somebody got away with it. That's the conclusion I won't accept."

Frank nodded and reached for his coffee. "I know," he said. "You won't let this go until you're satisfied you know the truth." He took a slow sip. "We're not there yet."

26.

Dale was back in his office with the door closed, sitting with Guy Tremblay. They had pushed their chairs away from the table leaving the paperwork spread out in front of them. They both looked uncomfortable with the subject under discussion and their part in the painful process of terminations.

"I know this is hard to do, Guy," said Dale. "I've worked with these people as long as you have, and I like them too. I don't want to see them lose their jobs and give them problems at home, but we have to make the hard decisions or we'll all lose our jobs. We have to be tough enough to make necessary changes and survive."

Guy grimaced. He had nothing to say.

Dale continued. "We have to reduce our technical staff by three and then add one or two with a better fit to support our new product lines. We've already talked about the need for a good mix of technical skills combined with the ability to explain the technology to customers. It's a very different business and a lot more demanding of technical support. We need more capable staff if we're going to succeed."

Guy leaned forward and put his elbows on the table to hold his head in his hands, staring at the paperwork on the table. He turned to Dale and said, "Do you want to have the new techs in place before we let these people go?"

"No, we can't afford to double up on staff, and it would be a bad start for them to be working with the people they're replacing. I'm hoping to start the new hires after we've paid the notice period and any severance to those who are leaving. When we're done, the payroll should be about the same as now, maybe a little less. We may be short-staffed for a while, but that's better than having higher payroll expense before we have the new revenue."

"*D'accord*," said Guy with a sigh. "We've agreed then. It's Jean-Marc, Roberto, and Theresa, right? So, when do you want to do this?"

"Yes, those are the three. We've spent enough time talking about it and trying to avoid it, we need to get on with it. The important thing now is to do this right. Let's look after those three as best we can, write up reference letters for each one and give them any referrals that might help them quickly find a new job. There's still lots of demand for their services, just not with us. I think we should do it Friday."

"*Mon Dieu.*" Guy looked down and started shuffling the papers in his folder as if he might find a different conclusion there. "That soon? This Friday?" Dale watched him digest the inevitable. Guy looked up and asked, "What about Patrick and the sales reps?"

Dale nodded. "He already let André and Paula go two months ago and now he's confirmed two new hires, including one experienced rep who is coming to us from corporate sales at Phoenix. Patrick will be giving notice to two more reps on Friday, the same time as you speak to the three techs."

"Maudit! C'est les mauvaises nouvelles partout."

"Oui, Guy, mais c'est les dernières, j'espère," said Dale. "I know it's a lot of bad news on Friday, but I'm hoping it's the last of it. I want everybody to know that I'm not planning any more bad news. No more layoffs for them to worry about. That's the message I want to be sure everybody gets before they go home and worry all weekend."

Guy looked concerned about the meetings they were going to have on Friday. "They're still going to worry all weekend. We'll have lots of questions to answer on Monday."

"We have to be sure we give everyone a clear message," said Dale. "The cutbacks and layoffs, restructuring, reorganisation—whatever you want to call it—we're done. Now we can get to work on our new plans. Starting Monday."

His expression showed grim determination. "Then it's do or die for all of us who are left. But first, we have to finish this process. I'll ask Marie and Monique to prepare the final paychecks for Friday including the remaining vacations, notice period and the severance pay they're entitled to. We'll have everything in envelopes and ready to hand to each of them."

Dale knew Marie and Monique Chevrier, his accountant and financial manager for 3D Computers, would be no more enthusiastic than Guy about seeing some of their fellow employees lose their jobs. It was a painful process and always provoked concerns that those remaining were not immune from the same unhappy conclusion. Marie and Monique, in particular, knew the business had been struggling. Their future was not guaranteed and was never going to be. Still, they knew what had to be done and wanted to be part of Dale's plans for the future, so they would try to make it as easy as they could for those who were leaving. This was not the first time in the past few months that cutbacks had been required. Layoffs and re-structuring were no surprise to anyone who was paying attention to the turmoil in the industry and the effects on other companies around them.

"Let's meet the three technicians together at two," said Dale. "We can tell them all the same thing at the same time, then help them pack up and leave before the end of the day. I know that seems cruel and insulting, like we don't trust them; but it's best to deliver the shock and then get out of each other's way. There's nothing gained by asking them to stay and work through the notice period. All that does is leave them here to argue about it and explain that we made a mistake and chose the wrong people. I would rather do the explaining to everyone myself after they're gone. Let them go home immediately so they can try to explain it to their families and start thinking about finding a new job."

"You're sure it's necessary for them to leave the same day? They'll feel like they got caught stealing or something and they're being thrown out for a reason they don't understand."

"I know. It's upsetting any way we do it. I'll try to

explain it to them when we meet, and I'm counting on you to help, Guy. Schedule a meeting with the rest of the department for the end of the day on Friday and we'll do our best to answer their questions before they go home for the weekend. On Monday morning we can cover it again for everybody in the staff meeting."

"*D'accord.* I guess you have a plan," said Guy. "We'll do it that way." He stood and started to gather up his papers.

"Thanks, Guy, I appreciate your support with all this." Dale reached out to give Guy a firm handshake. "I'm sure we'll get where we want to go after we get past this rough spot. I know it's hard."

He stood back and placed his notepad back on his desk. "I'm going out for lunch now, but I'll check in on you later this afternoon."

Above the noise of the traffic on Decarie Expressway outside the restaurant, Frank was taking a long look at the large plate of smoked-meat-on-rye with a sliced dill pickle beside it, a heap of fries with a packet of catsup and mayonnaise stuffed underneath, and a small paper cup of coleslaw on the side.

Dale had the same in front of him and said, "Looks good, eh? I thought you should join me here to compare the Snowdon Deli to your old favourite, Ben's Delicatessen, downtown. The smoked meat is good here too and it's a lot easier to get to from the West Island."

"I'll be fine with this," said Frank. He poked the meat

with his fork to push it back between the slices of rye bread and then picked it up in one hand. Dale would need two hands. Before biting into his sandwich, Frank asked, "So what's new with you, Dale? Your life must be more interesting than touring the smoked meat joints of Montreal. You've still got an unsolved murder on your hands and a business that's failing. All that should keep you busy."

"Lots going on these days," said Dale. "Not much progress on the murder, or suicide, whatever it is. Bobbie Brydon is definitely dead, but they still don't know for sure if he killed himself or somebody did it for him. Too many suspects and not enough proof to reach any conclusions yet."

He shifted in his seat and reached for his glass of Coca-Cola. "Some progress on the business side for me though. Still a slow and painful process. We're doing some layoffs this week and that's never easy for anybody. But we're turning the corner, I think. The new and improved 3D Computer Products is getting ready to kick ass. We're almost back to the roaring success we used to be."

"Good luck with that plan."

Dale laughed. "Yeah, right. I've gotta be optimistic, otherwise I'd give up."

"That might be a better plan for you," said Frank. "Wind it up, invest your money in something else, hang out on a beach in the Caribbean and write your memoirs. Or add a little drama and suspense to the real stories and write a bestseller."

"That's a tempting idea, but not yet. I want to leave

behind a success story that I can boast about to my kids, not tell them how I almost survived a crash landing but the business finally blew up in flames instead."

"That might work better to make your story a bestseller."

"I'm hoping that'll be the fiction, not the true story. I'm still counting on you to help me get to the happy ending of this story, Frank. Collecting from the deadbeats on my customer list has been very helpful. Any more cheques for me today?"

"Nothing today. But I have a couple of your deadbeats on notice to pay up by the end of the week, or else. They should be good for another forty grand. Then I'll need a new list of bad boys to squeeze for you. What about my suggestion of a little assistance from my friends with cash to help you out of this tight spot?"

"No thanks. Keep your friends to yourself. Speaking of which … any more threats from the Lucianos."

"I told you. They're done talking to me. If they have more to say they'll talk to you themselves. No news is good news."

"OK, I'll settle for that. I don't need the cash right now anyway. I'm managing to keep the bank friendly and helpful, pulling me back from the edge of the cliff. Most of the major creditors are co-operating and I've bought out a few that I don't need by offering them a discounted payment to wrap it up. Still a couple of tough nuts to crack, maybe you could do a little friendly persuasion with them."

"Sure. You know I can be very persuasive. Not always

friendly."

"Alright. Follow me back to the office after lunch and I'll give you a couple of names. See if you can persuade them to settle for a little less and leave me alone. Just don't go too far with your unfriendly tactics, I don't want to have to call my lawyer after the complaints start."

"What about the lawyers I suggested to you? I know you don't want Mafia money, but their lawyers are pretty good at keeping their clients out of trouble. I'm sure they'd be more creative and ambitious than the polite gentleman you're using now."

"I've had enough proposals from sleazy lawyers and bankruptcy trustees to know I don't want to go that route. I prefer to be known as a gentleman and work with other gentlemen. Except for you of course, Frank. You're my only exception."

"Gee, thanks. I'll take that as a compliment. But I think I need to start charging you more for the pleasure of doing business with me, unless you start taking me to better restaurants. You don't seem to know any of the fine dining establishments that Montreal is famous for."

"Ah, but I do. I'm saving them for when we have something to celebrate. Don't give up on me too soon."

27.

Hélène sat in the passenger seat beside Claude Samson in an unmarked blue four-door sedan parked in the street next to the driveway that curved past the two-car garage entrance and the stone steps at the front of Brydon's stone mansion. Samson leaned forward against the steering wheel and peered past Hélène to look at the house.

"Nice place," he said. "Is she expecting us?"

"No," said Hélène. "I didn't want to give her time to prepare for us. I'd rather see her first reaction to the tough questions. Might help us understand where the truth lies. Let's go see if she's home."

She got out and Samson followed her toward the front door. As they arrived together at the front steps, she turned and said, "I'll try to be polite. You can be the bad cop."

He shrugged. "That's usually my role. But I prefer tough cop—rough and tough maybe, but never a bad cop."

"Whatever you like," said Hélène. "In any case, she's not going to be very receptive to another visit. We already know she's a hostile witness. Let's find out if she's also our most likely suspect." They went up the steps and Hélène leaned on the doorbell.

Donna Brydon was not glad to see them, judging by the dark scowl looking out from the side window. She opened the door.

"What the hell do you want? I've got nothing new to say to you."

"Actually, we may have something new to say to you," said Hélène. "We have some new information we'd like to share with you and make sure we've got it right before we leap to any wrong conclusions."

Donna looked from one to the other, then asked Hélène, "Does he have to come in?"

Samson tried to look shocked but failed. He smiled at Hélène with his eyebrows twisted into a question mark.

Hélène said, "He'll behave. I've already asked him to be polite. But it's better if there's two of us to be sure we get the story straight."

Donna took another long moment to look from one to the other. "Come in off the front step," she said. "I really don't want the neighbours watching me getting grilled by two cops at my front door." She backed up to let them in and closed the door.

She hesitated before gesturing toward the living room, but it was going to be too crowded in the vestibule for a comfortable conversation. She indicated a large brown leather sofa where Claude and Hélène could sit side-by-side. She dropped her slim figure into the facing recliner in matching soft leather. She leaned back, crossed her legs and wrapped her arms around herself.

Hélène recognized the pose that Lisa must have learned from her mother.

Donna asked, "So what's new you want to talk to me about?"

"Thank you for giving us some time today," said Hélène. "I think it's important to keep you up to date and avoid any misunderstandings about what we know, and what we don't know yet. We've been speaking to the primary witnesses, your daughter Lisa and Dale Hunter, and some others who knew Mr. Brydon, but we're still trying to satisfy ourselves whether it was suicide or a homicide. There seem to be a lot of people who might have had a reason to want your husband dead."

She glanced sideways at Samson who was pre-occupied with looking around the living room at the ornate oversized brass lamps beside the walk-in-sized stone fireplace and the weird colourful splashes of modern art in wide black frames on the walls. He tilted his head and peered at the artwork to take a closer look, then shrugged and came back to the conversation.

Hélène continued, "As you know, the initial officers on the scene thought it looked suspicious, although Lisa and Hunter both still think it was a suicide."

"What the fuck," said Donna, looking at Samson. "You don't like my choice of art?"

"Uh, yeah, … no. It's great. But I'm no expert," said Samson, not looking at all embarrassed. "I don't have much art at home, just a few Playboy pin-ups hanging on the walls of my shabby apartment."

Equally unembarrassed, Donna shook her head in disgust.

She turned to Hélène. "You need to let it go. There was

no murder. It was suicide. He had a lot going on that he couldn't handle and he was looking for an easy way out. So he shot himself. You're not going to find anything to conclude otherwise. You must have something better to do than trying to solve a murder that didn't happen."

"We do have a few other cases where we know for sure it was murder, this one we still need to decide," said Hélène. "You know the reasons we're suspicious about your husband's death as a suicide—the gun in his right hand, no prints on the trigger, no suicide note, and no one seems to have been aware of any prior thoughts he might have had about killing himself. Those questions still exist and lead us to wonder if he was killed, who might have motive? Who would benefit from his death?"

"So you come to my house uninvited, and you're accusing *me* of his fucking murder?"

"We're not accusing anybody yet," said Hélène.

"But if we accused anybody, you'd be the first fucking suspect," said Samson. "You had the most to gain from his death."

Both women sucked in their breath and looked wide-eyed at Samson.

Hélène slowly turned back to Donna, "It's true, you clearly had motive and you *have* benefited from his death, but you're not the only one with motive. There were a lot of angry people after his bankruptcy who might have wanted revenge and we're looking into that, of course. I understand Mr. Brydon owed a lot of money to your family too."

"My family?" Donna gave Hélène a hard look and dared her to continue.

"Yes. Your cousin, Tony Luciano, in particular. He has a couple of different companies that never got paid what they were owed by Mr. Brydon's company and it added up to over two million dollars."

Donna Brydon sat back in her chair, clasped her hands together and brought them up against her chin to look at Hélène. She ignored Samson. "I don't know anything about that."

"You never talked to Tony about any business he was doing with your husband?"

"No." She continued to look straight at Hélène.

Samson spoke up. "Did you ever talk to him about helping you get the divorce settlement you wanted from your husband?"

She continued looking at Hélène and clenched her jaw.

Samson added, "I hear Tony is a pretty good negotiator. Maybe you asked him to do whatever it takes to get more out of Bobbie. He's known for tactics that are hard to say no to."

Donna turned and glared at him. "You fucking asshole. I thought she told you to be polite. Leave my fucking family out of this."

Hélène interrupted the two of them locked in competing glares. "We can't really ignore the family connection," she said. "Some of the trails lead back to you and to them. Let me ask you again, more politely. Did you ask your cousin,

Tony Luciano, or anyone else in the family to intervene in your divorce settlement with Mr. Brydon? To put pressure on him on your behalf?"

Donna looked back at Hélène. "And I'm telling you just as fucking politely, no. I did not."

She leaned forward and glared once more at Samson before returning to Hélène. "They knew I was getting nowhere with my useless fucking husband and they're very protective of the family. They knew I was ready to kill him for trying to screw me out of what he owed me. But I never ever asked them to do it for me."

She slumped back into the recliner and clasped her arms around herself again, scowling at the floor between Hélène and Claude. After a moment, she released her arms, shrugged and leaned forward with her hands clasped in her lap.

She looked up and turned from Hélène to Claude and back to Hélène.

She said, "Maybe they misunderstood."

28.

The two detectives were back at Station 21. Hélène had done her notes in the car during the fifteen-minute drive back down the hillside from Westmount into downtown. She was on the phone in her office and put it down just as Claude stuck his head in the door. He shuffled in and stood in front of Hélène's desk.

He had asked her earlier in the car, "What did you make of that?"

Hélène had replied, "I think she just directed us toward her cousin, Tony Luciano." Now in her office, she looked up at Claude as he came in.

"You already on the phone to Tony?" he asked.

"Haven't called him yet. I don't have him on speed dial."

"We better do our homework before we make that call."

"Yeah, that's for sure," said Hélène. "He won't be as polite as Donna Brydon when he tells us to fuck off. Come in and take a load off, Claude, we need to talk about approaching Tony Luciano."

Claude flopped into one of the flimsy visitor chairs. "Of course Tony would never do it himself," he said. "It would always be one of his henchmen while he ensured he had a good alibi. But I don't see one of his hired guns doing it so badly. Like you said before, they'd either do a better job of the fake suicide or make it clear it was an execution to send a message. Fumbling this fucked-up suicide just doesn't seem like a professional hit arranged by somebody like Tony Luciano."

"Maybe they asked an amateur to do it for them. Maybe Donna asked them to show her how to do it and she didn't follow instructions very well."

Claude looked skeptical. "You think Brydon would let her into his office with a gun in her hand?"

"I think she'd be smarter than that," said Hélène. "He could have let her in on some pretense, then boom, she gets him with a gun he never saw. She's still the number one suspect for me. We need to figure out where that gun came from. Was it Bobbie's or somebody else's? Donna pointing the finger at her cousin Tony is just too easy for her to send us in another direction. She knows we're always suspicious of Tony doing dirty deeds, but I don't think this is going to lead anywhere. Anyway, we can't just walk in on him and start testing theories like we did with Donna Brydon. His lawyers will be claiming harassment again. We'll have to dig deeper and find some reason to question him."

"I could call on him. No problem," said Claude.

"Still working on your tough guy reputation, Claude? Tony Luciano might be a good test for you." She laughed. "Let's leave it alone until we have a little more to work with before we poke the bear."

Claude shrugged. "Not sure where we look next," he said. "You told me that Frank knows his driver, Vinnie Mancuso. Maybe they could have a little chat. Frank's good at learning stuff the Lucianos and their friends will never tell us. Not sure what he gives them in return, but it seems they have an understanding and they try to use him as intermediary when they think it helps their cause. Maybe Frank can find out more about what's going on between Tony Luciano and Donna Brydon. Something we don't know about yet."

"Yeah, I haven't heard from Frank lately but he's been trying to check out that angle," said Hélène. "I'm sure he'll let me know if he learns anything interesting. What about those companies on Brydon's creditors list and the other names that Dale Hunter gave us? Anything worth looking at there?"

"Nothing so far. They're all legit as far as I can tell. Businessmen who don't usually kill their customers over some bad debt. They might break up some furniture I'm told, maybe yell at the wife and kids, kick the dog, but otherwise fine upstanding citizens."

"No murderers?"

"Not that I found."

"Do we have any other lists?"

"Nope. We're running out of suspects. Maybe have to accept it as a suicide and remove the suspicious death label. Donna will be happy to have us release the death certificate so she can collect the insurance. Did you hear it's worth five million?"

"That's worth killing him for."

"You're back to that?"

"Yeah. Let's not sign off on that death certificate yet. Still a suspicious death for me."

"OK, boss. We'll keep working on it." Claude hefted himself up and went to the door. "You want it closed?"

"Yes, please," said Hélène. She leaned forward to pick up her phone again. She was thinking it was time to compare notes with Frank and hear his thoughts on the Lucianos and the potential murderers in the family.

29.

Dale was at home in the evening with Susan at the kitchen table. They had cleared the dishes after dinner and were sitting quietly chatting. The kids had gone upstairs to finish their homework before going to bed. Dale was giving Susan an update on the latest news at work and the recent briefing from Frank. "You really think the Mafia are threatening you again?" she asked.

"No, not really. Frank had a chat with them and I'm sure they're not concerned about me with all the other shit they're into. I don't feel threatened, but I think maybe Lisa needs a warning. She's the one who suggested Tony Luciano might be involved and I gave Hélène and Samson the business card with his note on it. They'll decide what to do with it and I'm sure they'll keep their sources confidential, whether it's me or Lisa. They know Luciano can be dangerous if he knows who's working against him."

"Surely the Lucianos wouldn't do anything to harm Lisa would they? Isn't she part of the family they're trying to protect?"

"That's true. But they value loyalty to the family more than anything and they are likely to fix it pretty quick if they get the impression someone in the family is leaking their secrets. I'm sure Lisa has been around them long enough to know that. She's a bright kid and pretty street wise, I'd say. She's Brydon's daughter and loyal to him first, I'm sure, but she knows enough about her mother's family. She's not naïve. She knows who they are and how they operate."

They were interrupted by the doorbell ringing. Dale glanced at his watch and frowned. He pushed away from the table and got up to go to the door. *Door-to-door salesman spoiling my evening? Maybe I should listen to his pitch and see if he's any good. We're still looking for salesmen. Maybe somebody selling air-duct cleaning or encyclopedias can be re-trained to sell computer products.*

"Sorry," said Susan, "that'll be Lawrence from next door. I forgot to warn you. I told him to drop in after dinner. He's looking for your advice again."

"Really? More issues with his lawncare business? I was hoping Sean was going to work for him again this summer. It's good for him, a little fresh air and exercise away from the computer keyboard. He even earns a few bucks while he's at it."

"No, it's not about his lawncare business. Lawrence told me he wants to talk to you about his plans for college and university. He finishes high school this year and he's not sure what to do next."

"Oh, OK." Dale headed for the front door. "I'll talk to him, but I need to be careful I don't contradict his parents. I wonder what they have in mind for him."

After Lawrence left, the kids were in bed and the house was quiet. Dale cleaned up in the kitchen, started the dishwasher and turned the lights out, then joined Susan in the family room.

She was sitting with a glass of white wine on the table and a book in her hands. The front showed a covered bridge in lush green countryside with the title, *The Bridges of Madison County*. Dale didn't like the idea she was reading a story about a married woman having an affair, but it had been on the best-seller lists for over a year, so she had to read it. Dale had refilled his after-dinner coffee and set it on the low table between them, waiting for Susan to look up. She put her book down under the lamp on the small table beside her armchair. "You looked after Lawrence all right?"

"He's a bright kid and should do well in business someday. He's still trying to decide what to study and where to start. Science and engineering or finance and economics? At McGill or Concordia? Or somewhere else away from home.

"Remember those days, Sue, back when we had to make the same decisions before going to UBC? We were both happy to leave our hometowns and head off to the big city, but I don't think Lawrence's parents want to see him leave. Montreal has lots of choices for universities, which is good for the parents, but not so good for the kids who want to get away from home. That's such an important part of the university experience; but I didn't want to step on that landmine."

"But you still had some answers for him, right?"

"I tried to give him some direction in the process. No

answers."

"I'm sure you told him your preference for running a business and being your own boss instead of getting into big business?"

"I told him the differences I see based on my experience in both. He'll make up his own mind. Like I tell everyone, find what you like and what you're good at, and choose that. They don't always go together. You may be good at something you don't like and not good at something you do like. As you know, I would've liked to be a rock star or a hockey hero, but wasn't good enough at either. I also wasn't very good at engineering and science, so I chose a career in business and management which I liked better and discovered later I was pretty good at. Not my original career plan, but a lot of my plans changed at UBC."

He smiled at Susan as they both reflected on their times together at university in Vancouver where they first met. "And the best part was meeting you, of course." Two small-town kids in the big city, they fell in love and got married before moving to Montreal, where Dale had been accepted into the MBA program at McGill.

"Like I said, Lawrence is a bright kid, he'll make good decisions," said Dale. "He's already decided he doesn't want to make a career in landscaping, but he does like the challenges of running a business. He'll do alright. Especially if he gets a good education."

"You'll have to share that advice with Sean," said Susan. "You think he'll follow in your footsteps and run his own business someday?"

"Maybe, but he gets more excited by the technology than the business side. He's more interested in computer science than entrepreneurship."

Susan smiled and nodded to herself. She took a sip of wine and put down her glass. "Enough about the kids, let's talk about the adults."

Dale looked intrigued and faked a shy smile.

She got up and came over to him and reached for his hands to pull him up to her. She placed one of his hands gently on the breast that was still tender from the surgery.

"I want you to touch me," she said. "Make love to me."

Dale leaned forward and kissed her on the forehead. "I was waiting for the invitation." Susan took his hand in hers and led him out of the room toward the stairs and up to their bedroom.

"You're invited," she said.

30.

Dale looked up from his desk at the office the next morning and saw a large black Mercedes with dark-tinted windows pull in off the service road, and park outside the front of 3D Computer Products. He watched as the bulky middle-aged driver got out of the car. He filled his black suit, wore no tie, white shirt open at the neck, and his jacket swung open as he closed the driver's door and went around to the other side. He opened the rear passenger door and another man got out. Slim, mid-forties with curly dark hair showing some grey, he was in an immaculate sleek blue suit and white shirt with a red silk tie. He pulled the cuffs out straight and buttoned the jacket before speaking to his driver, then they walked together to the front door.

A few minutes later, Marie came down the hall and into Dale's office. She spoke softly, "Two guys just arrived. The one who looks like the boss asked to see you." She handed Dale a business card. "He says he's a friend of the family and wants to talk to you about Bobbie Brydon."

Dale looked at the card and realized he had seen it before. It showed the name of Anthony Luciano, President of Agile Construction, with an address on Wellington Street West in Verdun, a suburb in southwest Montreal. He quickly checked the other side of the card. There was no note.

"All right, bring them in," he said. He was remembering Frank's warning. *You don't want Tony Luciano to deliver the message himself.*

Marie escorted them down the hall to Dale's office, and after a firm handshake, Tony Luciano made himself comfortable in the chair in front of Dale's desk. He did not introduce the driver. Dale assumed it was Vinnie Mancuso, who remained standing by the door that he had closed behind them after Marie left. He buttoned his jacket and held his hands together in front.

Dale looked at the dark-haired man seated with his hands laced calmly in his lap. Luciano leaned back with his stretched-out legs crossed at the ankles and Dale noticed his shoes—soft brown leather in a woven pattern ending at the smooth pointed toe caps. *Sharp-dressed man with a big Mercedes limousine and a bodyguard opening doors for him. Maybe I should get out of computers and into the construction business. Except it's probably more dangerous and more corrupt than what I'm doing now. Not really what I'm looking for next.*

"Mr. Hunter," said Luciano, "I thought we should have a chat. We're both businessmen, so I think we'll understand each other. Neither of us likes any interference in our business, right?"

Dale let him wait for a moment, then said, "Sure, what did you want to chat about?"

"I think you know already. Our mutual friend, Frank, he told you." Luciano paused, and added, "We don't want you working with the police on Bobbie Brydon's death." His face hardened as he waited for Dale to absorb that message.

"Seriously, Hunter, you need to back off. Do not help them investigate his death as a murder. Do not suggest his wife had anything to do with it. And don't *ever* suggest my family had anything to do with it. I don't need the cops interfering with my business any more than they do already. And you don't want me interfering with *your* business. Is that clear enough for you?"

"I get it," said Dale. "Absolutely."

"You need to take this seriously," said Tony, his face darkened further. "You seem a little too casual to me." He looked over his shoulder at Mancuso, who stood staring at Dale.

Luciano added, "You know if you don't stay out of this, we'll have to remove you ourselves, right?"

Dale shifted in his chair. "Yes, I understand that. Message received."

Tony Luciano sat still and looked into Dale's eyes for a long moment.

Then he stood and said, "Good. I knew this meeting wouldn't take long. You're a bright guy, Hunter. Take care of yourself." There was a flicker of a smirk as he turned to the door. "*Bonne journée*, have a good day." Mancuso opened it and they both left the office.

Dale sat back to look out his window and watch them walk out to their car. As they pulled away and drove out of sight down the highway, he let out a long breath.

Brief and to the point. 'Or we'll have to remove you ourselves.'

Very persuasive, this sharp-dressed man.

31.

Hélène was in her office which always seemed smaller with Claude Samson in it. "So you decided to make a call on Luciano yesterday," she said.

"Yeah," said Claude. "Figured it couldn't hurt to include him in our research, just ask a few questions. Politely, of course. Carney came along to keep me in line."

"Shit. He's worse than you with the tough guy routine."

"Nah, we're both very smooth when we have to be. Luciano was a gentleman, too. He knows how to put on the good guy act himself. We had a very pleasant chat."

"I'm glad to hear it, but what did you learn that'll help us wrap up this Bobbie Brydon case."

Well," said Claude, looking very pleased with himself. "I'm happy to report that Luciano says he didn't do it."

Hélène didn't look impressed.

Claude continued, "I know that's not a surprise to you, but he claimed Brydon didn't owe them enough to kill him for it. Not that he would ever do that, of course. I didn't tell him we had his business card with a threatening note on it and an amount that even I'd be willing to kill for."

Hélène asked, "What did he have to say about Donna Brydon."

"I did ask him about Mrs. Brydon, and I have to admit that Carney provoked him a bit on that score. He asked if Tony had whacked Bobbie to get her the insurance, since the divorce settlement wasn't going so well. That hit a nerve for Tony."

"I'll bet."

"So he ranted about us wasting his time with a bullshit murder investigation. He did know about the insurance, and he told us to just sign off on the damn suicide, so Donna could settle his estate and claim the insurance. Myself, I think there's something there. Maybe a deal between Tony and her to give him half the five million she'll get in insurance. That would pay off the debt that Bobbie owed plus a small bonus for his services, whatever they were."

"Unfortunately, it's still just a theory." said Hélène. "You may be right, but we need more than that to come back at him."

"It's the best we can do on a first visit," said Claude. "Don't worry, we're not done with him yet. Pat's talking to the insurance company and the bank to let them both know we're still suspicious. He's asking for a search warrant to monitor Donna's bank account so we can trace the money after she gets it and see if she sends any of it to Tony or a known Luciano account. With his history of money laundering and extortion it should be an easy ask."

"It's something," said Hélène. "Small progress after six weeks, but it's something."

She stood up behind her desk. "I've got another interview to supervise, Claude. That's all for now, thanks." She walked out of her office, followed by Claude, who went out to the cluster of desks in the open area to look for Detective Pat Carney. They all had more work to do.

32.

Back at the office, Dale was on the phone with Rick Petrie. "I know it's still tight," he said, "but I've settled with most of the overdue accounts now and the remaining suppliers are putting me back on regular terms again. So the cashflow is back under control, and revenue is going up with the new orders being shipped. I've also got some really significant sales in the works that should be confirmed this week. You can relax, Rick, the bank has nothing to worry about."

It was only a slight exaggeration, not lying really—just improving on the truth. Dale figured it was his job to worry and keep the bank from doing it for him. Rick Petrie had stuck his neck out and arranged to extend the bank financing, though, so Dale didn't want to let him down. And he was optimistic that he was on the right track and pulling away from the disaster of a failing business.

His priority today was a joint presentation with Jean-Guy Brassard of Phoenix Systems to a new supplier of mass storage devices whose sales team was flying in from San José, California. The data storage market was growing fast and Dale and Jean-Guy wanted to double-team them and show they could deliver the one-two punch for distribution and sales to justify exclusive rights for all of Canada for their full product line. It was a huge opportunity for both Dale and Jean-Guy, and they had done their homework to prepare a thorough and impressive pitch. Patrick Jensen and Guy Tremblay were standing by to do the tour of the newly refurbished and re-equipped premises of 3D Computer Products and introduce the visitors to the sales and technical staff.

Dale placed the acetate slides into the folder to go and test the overhead projector set up in the conference room. The meeting with the supplier was scheduled after a gourmet lunch they had arranged in historic Old Montreal to loosen them up beforehand. That always worked, and for American suppliers in particular, exposing them to the French language and culture was a convincing argument to persuade them they couldn't possibly deal with *Québec* and the rest of Canada without a strong bilingual team for sales and support.

As he was about to leave his office, Dale saw Monique Chevrier coming down the hall toward him. Monique was an attractive young woman who had worked for Dale for almost eight years now and was one of his most competent and trusted employees. They had developed a close personal relationship of mutual confidence and trust that made her an effective partner in his business and Dale relied on her through good times and bad. She closely monitored financial performance and delivered early warnings of any problems before they got worse. She also knew how to report the good news with as much embellishment as they could get away with to maintain the support of the bank. Some might have presumed there was more to their personal relationship than being trusted confidants, but there was never any hint of unbusinesslike conduct from either of them.

Monique stepped in and closed Dale's office door behind her. "I reviewed the letter you gave me with Paul Macrae," she said. "He agreed we can't just ignore it; we have to reply."

"And he thinks Theresa Leblanc has a case in asking for a full year's salary in severance pay? Or getting her job back?"

Monique placed the document back in the large manila envelope and put it on the conference table for Dale. "Well, he didn't say she had a case. He said we have to reply and make our case against her claims. Aside from wrongful dismissal, meaning termination without cause, she is also claiming discrimination against her as a female based on the fact she had more seniority than some of the male techs who got to keep their jobs."

"She knows that's not true!" He was shaking his head in frustration. "We explained to all of them that we needed to replace some of our techs with others who had more expertise related to the new product lines. It had nothing to do with their performance or seniority, and certainly not because Theresa is a woman. We've never discriminated against female employees and always met our obligations for pay equity."

"Paul knows that and he agrees that you should be able to defend yourself against her claims, but Theresa's good performance reviews and the recommendations in your reference letter for her don't help your case much. Apparently, Theresa was coached by Lisa to defend herself and she recommended this lawyer who's building a reputation as a defender of women's rights. She wants to take it on a contingency basis, for her fees to be paid only if she wins a settlement. If it goes before an activist judge who also supports the feminist cause, you may have a problem."

"Did you speak to Theresa yourself?"

"No, I didn't," said Monique. "But she called Guy to let him know the lawyer's letter was coming and tried to find out if anything had changed since she left."

"I hope Guy was careful with what he said. We don't need to give her lawyer more ammunition to shoot back at us."

"He didn't tell her anything she didn't already know. But Guy also gave her a glowing reference letter that they might use against us."

"Shit, we try to do the right thing and then the lawyers get in the middle and mess it up for everybody. Talk to Paul and ask him to draft a reply. Meanwhile, I'll try to speak to Theresa myself and ask her to come in and discuss it. Her lawyer will probably tell her not to speak to me, but maybe we can work it out between us without any lawyers involved."

He took the envelope from the conference table and placed it on top of his inbox. "Thanks, Monique. I appreciate you and Guy both trying to avoid making this mess worse than it needs to be."

Meanwhile, in the industrial district by the Lachine canal on Wellington Street, Frank the Fixer was parked in his black Caddy outside the front entrance to Agile Construction. Behind the low red-brick office building was a barbed-wire-topped chain-link fence around a parking lot filled with Agile Construction trucks and heavy equipment. In front there was a row of empty visitor parking spaces, but Frank had parked down the street away from the building where he could watch the entrance. He saw the familiar black limo pull in near the front door and stop to let Tony Luciano get out and go into the building. Frank watched as Vinnie Mancuso drove around the back to park.

Mancuso was walking out from the back lot to the front door when Frank approached him. "Hey, Vinnie, can I buy you a coffee? We need to chat for a couple of minutes."

"Hi, Frank. Sure, you can always buy me a coffee. That was my next stop anyway." Mancuso thumbed toward the coffee truck that was double-parked at the end of the street. "We can chat there. The coffee's better at the office, but you probably don't want to come inside and I don't want to chat with you there either."

"I'm willing to settle for that," said Frank. "I'm not that fussy. Coffee's coffee."

He turned and they walked together back down the street to the coffee truck. "Maybe you'd like something for your sweet tooth to make up for the bad coffee." Frank gestured at the display of pre-packaged pastries and sandwiches under the awning that was propped up by an aluminum bar at the side of the truck.

"Jesus, Frank, you're a bad influence," said Mancuso. "You trying to spoil my figure?" Mancuso's ample belly contradicted his claim to any concerns about his figure. He nodded to the attendant who reached for Mancuso's regular choice, a two-pack of chocolate croissants.

"Thanks, Frank," he said, accepting a large black coffee and stepping away from the truck where they couldn't be seen from the office or heard by anyone else on the sidewalk waiting to be served. Frank handed the attendant a ten-dollar bill and waved off the change before joining Mancuso with his own large black coffee. He took a sip as Mancuso asked, "So what's on your mind, Frank?"

"Same as last time," said Frank. "The Bobbie Brydon suicide we were talking about."

"Ah, that shit again. I got nothing new for you, Frank. The police are still fucking around trying to prove it was not a suicide and your friend, Hunter, is still sticking his nose into it even after you warned him about it. Tony was pissed about it. He chatted to Hunter this morning. He might need one more little chat before Tony decides to do something more serious. I don't know why he's so easy on him. Hunter doesn't seem to listen anyway. Stubborn fucker, isn't he?"

"Yeah, he insists on doing it his way. I don't think he's interfering though, just trying to make sure the police get it right and don't come back at him for any part of it."

"Yeah, I know. He seems worried about the police. He

needs to be more worried about Tony."

"I'll remind him. And what do *you* think, Vinnie? Any chance Brydon might have been murdered?"

Mancuso took a long sip of his coffee. "It wasn't Tony. But what does it matter anyway? The sonofabitch deserved to die. Murder or suicide, who cares? That poor woman …" He shook his head. "She put up with all his shit. He deserved to die."

"You knew Bobbie and his wife yourself?"

"Yeah, I knew 'em both. She complained to Tony a lot and I was usually there. Beautiful woman, really. She deserved better than the way that asshole treated her. She wanted him dead, I know that, so … if he didn't do it to himself, somebody else had to do it."

Mancuso raised his eyebrows at Frank and left the question mark hanging in the air. Then he asked, "And how are you doing with your lady friend at the cop shop, Frank? She must be keeping you up to date on what's happening. Dunno why you're asking me."

"Just trying to keep everybody onside," said Frank. "Making sure we've all got the story straight."

Vinnie shrugged. "Be careful playing that game, Frank. Like Johnny Cash, you gotta walk the line." He bobbed his head. "Keep your eyes wide open all the time." He smiled. Without singing it, he did get the rhythm right.

"Who's Johnny Cash?" Frank smiled back. "Doesn't sound Italian."

"You gotta start hanging out in some different bars,"

said Vinnie.

They finished their coffee, tossed the cups in a garbage bag hanging at a corner of the coffee truck and went their separate ways after a firm, friendly handshake.

Vinnie went up the steps to the front door of Agile Construction and stopped to watch Frank drive off. He was smiling and shaking his head at Frank's manoeuvring between the players, 'to get the story straight.'

Back in the Caddy, Frank kept his eyes on the traffic as he collected his thoughts and prepared to share them with Dale and Hélène.

PART 3

TWISTED TRAILS

33.

Three weeks later, back at Station 21, Claude Samson and Pat Carney were seated facing each other over their shared desktops. Carney had his feet up on the corner of his desk and Samson was leaning back in his chair, feet crossed under the desk, and he asked, "So what've we got to report to Hélène at this point? She's looking for progress and wants to know when we can wrap this up. Brydon's death, murder or suicide; it's taking up too much of our time."

"Yeah, I agree. I think we can park it on the back burner for a while," said Carney. "We've finished with all the leads we had, and we've set the traps for somebody to take the bait and incriminate themselves. We can sit and wait for that to happen now."

"Not sure she's gonna like the idea we're doing nothing but waiting for somebody else to do something. She's got the problem of having to decide whether the death was a suicide or a murder. Suicide is not a problem for us; there's no murderer to look for and arrest. But calling it a suicide now seems like the easy way to close it and she doesn't want anybody to think we were too lazy, or too busy, or too incompetent to prove it was a murder."

"But we've followed up on every lead and investigated every possible scenario," said Carney. "We still don't have any proof of murder. And nothing sufficient to suggest

Donna Brydon or anyone else was responsible for Brydon's death. That's what we told the insurance company and they had to pay out what they owed her. She might have killed him to get it, but we can't prove it. We're monitoring her accounts and if she transfers a bundle of that money to Tony Luciano, we'll have something more to go after her with."

"I know all that," said Samson. "I'm not satisfied either that we've gotten to the truth yet. There are a lot of people with motive and opportunity who are also smart and tough enough to cover it up. They're not likely to be stupid enough to step into the traps we've set for them. I think somebody out there is probably going to get away with murder."

"That would be a shitty way to have it end. Unsolved crimes unit trying again in twenty years? I'm not waiting that long." Carney shifted in his chair and glared at the file folder on Samson's desk. "You know one guy who's getting off too easy?"

He waited for Samson to look up. "Hunter," he said. "I'd like to push his buttons a little harder. He just seems too good to be true. A little too smooth, I think. Explaining it all away. Everybody just accepts that it couldn't be him. Too nice a guy to kill anybody. That's what they all say after we discover who's actually the killer in cases like this."

"Pat, are you forgetting Hélène knows him pretty well? She was the first to accept his story. She's convinced he's an innocent bystander."

"Yeah, I know that, but didn't you tell me he got

involved with organized crime in the past?"

"Yeah, but he was the victim," said Samson. "He got caught up in extortion and money laundering, but he was never part of the Mob himself. They gave him no choice and threatened his family to keep him in line. He eventually got out from under, but it wasn't easy."

"OK, so they already know his hot buttons and how to get him onside. Maybe they persuaded him to co-operate again. Maybe it wasn't Donna Brydon persuading Tony Luciano to kill Bobbie, it was Tony Luciano persuading Dale Hunter to kill him. Hunter didn't have motive, but they did. And Hunter had easy access to Bobbie any time."

Samson ran his large hand up into his hair and pushed it back off his forehead.

"Jesus, the last thing we need is another fucking theory to chase down," he said. "Look, Pat, you need to visit Hunter yourself and decide if this is worth pursuing or not."

"You think Hélène will be OK with that?"

"Yeah, but do it soon and we'll tell her after you have something more than a hopeful hunch. She'd want to be sure we never hesitated for a minute just because she knows Hunter and his family. She wants us to do our job and check up on all the possible suspects, whoever they are." Carney nodded, grabbed his brown-check sports jacket and shrugged it on to leave the department.

Samson continued. "Speaking of suspects, though, you've reminded me to go see Luciano again. I have a few new questions for him, maybe he has some new answers.

You go ahead with Hunter, and I'll check in on Tony tomorrow."

Before Carney got far from the desk, Samson added, "There's also some additional forensic evidence I asked for. We should have a look at that before we talk to anybody."

Carney came back to lean on Samson's side of the desk. "What's that?" he asked.

"Well, we already checked fingerprints on the gun Brydon was killed with and found only his. The wrong hand maybe, but only his. Now we have a long list of suspects who might have placed that loaded gun in his hand. Hélène's boyfriend Frank added Luciano's driver to the list, Vinnie Mancuso, since he apparently has the hots for Donna Bryon, and you just added Dale Hunter again."

Carney leaned back. "So?"

"So, if Brydon loaded the gun himself, his fingerprints should be on the bullet casings in the gun and on the one ejected onto the floor beside him. If there are none, or somebody else's fingerprints are on the shell casings, then we might have some new evidence to ask the right people some new questions. I asked the lab to take a closer look. It was never a priority because we thought we knew all we needed to know. Soon we may know a little more. I'll call the lab tomorrow and see if they've got anything yet."

Carney was nodding and rubbing his chin. "What about looking for DNA evidence? That seems to be all the lab wants to find these days. The forensic analysis is getting better apparently, and they can pick up identifiable DNA from microscopic traces. The prosecutors love to have that kind of evidence and they're getting used to it nailing the case closed for us."

"Yeah, our lab is still catching up with the technology, but they told me they'll take a closer look for any DNA traces too."

"Could be interesting," said Carney. "We could use some solid evidence leading us in the right direction." He turned from the open office and headed toward the hallway and stairs to exit.

"We'll see," said Samson to himself. He didn't look that optimistic.

34.

Dale and Susan were seated at a round table for two on the raised patio at the back of Le Village restaurant looking out across the immaculately tended lawn and flower gardens toward the river. The mid-summer evening was comfortably warm and the setting sun behind the restaurant reflected a red-tinted glow on the tall maple and birch trees along the banks of the broad Ottawa River that stretched in front of them and flowed in smooth dark swirls into the widening waters of the Lake of Two Mountains before joining the Saint Lawrence River at the west end of the island of Montreal.

"I think it's a significant milestone worth celebrating," said Dale. "It's been three months since your surgery and the chemo treatment is finished now too. Your last check-up showed no signs of any cancer. Aren't you ready to relax and enjoy the pleasures of fine dining in a romantic spot for a change? It's been a while."

"Yes, I'm ready to relax and the cancer scare seems to be over. I hope it's gone for good. I'm actually more worried about Sean and Keira being home alone babysitting themselves for the first time tonight."

Dale laughed. "I think we're OK. Now that Sean's fourteen, it's legal and nobody is going to report us for being bad parents. I already checked-in from the car and

I can call them every fifteen minutes if you like."

Susan smiled. "Every hour should be enough. Sean is taking it very seriously. I just hope he doesn't get carried away with bossing Keira around."

"They'll be fine. Let's get back to taking care of you."

Dale put down his wine glass and checked that the waiter was not yet coming to take their orders. He left the open menu beside his plate to deter any interruption. "Let me say something first, Susan." He reached for her hand and held it in his. "I'm really sorry your health concerns came at such a bad time for me and the business. I know I didn't give you enough time and attention when you needed it most. I'm really sorry about that."

"No, no, Dale. You don't have to apologize at all. I know there was a lot going on for you at work and it wasn't all under your control. Plus, it was compounded by Bobbie's death at the office. I know you have to juggle priorities and I never feel like you're neglecting me or the family. Sometimes you just have too much coming at you all at the same time."

"That's very understanding and very forgiving of you," said Dale. "That's part of why I love you so much." He coughed softly into his napkin to clear the emotions rising in his throat. "I still think I could have done better and you should take advantage of me trying to make it up to you. That's why we're here." He gestured across the lawn to the view of the water and the pink and mauve clouds reflecting the sunset behind them.

Susan smiled and squeezed his hand. "I appreciate it and I'll do my best to take advantage of you."

"Good, let's see if we can find all your favourites—for the starter, main course and dessert." He picked up the large leather-bound menu and Susan reached for hers.

"Let's not get too carried away," she said. "We have the rest of the summer to enjoy outdoor dining. Might be fun to include the kids sometime too. Then I won't be worrying about what's going on at home while we're out."

"Set that aside for now. Concentrate on the menu. There are a lot of good choices."

They did enjoy their evening with a very good meal and even neglected calling the kids. They knew Sean had the number of the restaurant if he needed them. Dale was beginning to re-think his stubborn refusal to upgrade his mobile phone from the one attached to the console in his car and buying one of the newer portable models that he could carry with him. That would certainly be more practical in situations like this.

After the sun had gone down, they were still comfortably seated on the patio deck under the lights and lingered over their remaining glasses of wine and plates of dessert. They had both enjoyed their crème caramel, and Dale had ordered a cappuccino with dessert. Susan was appreciating a final glass of red wine.

"It's really good to see you recovering so well, Susan. How are you finding the yoga classes and the tennis now that you're back to the gym and tennis club again?"

"It's great," said Susan. "I'm out of shape after doing so little for all that time with the surgery and chemo, but my energy and fitness are coming back. In fact, I'm getting bored with too much time on my hands and looking for more to keep me going. I was even thinking I could come into the office and help out while the kids are away at summer camp for the next three weeks."

"Hey, that would be great. We haven't seen you at the office for a few years and Marie could use your help again. She's really overloaded since we cut back on some of the admin staff. She's not very good at neglecting the paperwork, regardless of how many times I tell her we don't need to do it all. Unfortunately, the government demands to fill out forms and send in reports are getting worse instead of better. Too many bureaucrats with too much time on their hands finding new ways to waste our time."

Susan ignored his brief rant. "It'll be fun, and a change in routine for me too. Good to get my brain engaged again with some new challenges. I'll take a look at my schedule and let you know when I can come in. Maybe even find a few days when the kids are away at camp and I can come in with you and stay until you leave."

"Now, I'm feeling guilty again. This was supposed to be a relaxing break for you and instead you get recruited into coming to work at the office again."

"It was my idea, remember? And it's always been our family business, right? Sometimes the family has to recognize that priorities shift to the business first. Besides you can relieve your guilt by paying for dinner. That should make you feel better."

She nodded toward the small leather folder placed by the waiter on the corner of their table with *l'addition* neatly folded inside so only Dale could see the amount when he opened it.

"You're right," he said, opening the leather folder and looking at the bill. "I know we're not keeping score, but this should get me a little closer to even."

35.

On Monday morning, Dale Hunter backed out of the driveway from his house in the quiet West Island suburb of Beaconsfield. He headed out of the neighbourhood toward St. Charles Boulevard north to Autoroute 40 and then east toward the city and his office on the south service road. It was seven-fifteen. There were others leaving for work at that time of the morning, heading to the train station, or into the traffic for the commute to downtown and the commercial and industrial developments around the city.

He didn't notice the large, black limousine that had been parked across the street from his house and followed him out to St. Charles Boulevard. It pulled up beside him at the first traffic lights and the tinted front passenger side window slid down. Dale looked over and recognized Tony Luciano's driver, Vinnie Mancuso, at the wheel. He gestured for Dale to pull into the strip mall parking lot immediately ahead on his right. Dale hesitated as the light changed to green. *What the hell does he want? I thought I was done with these guys.*

There was not much choice, so he pulled into the parking lot and Mancuso followed. The limo pulled in beside Dale, facing in the opposite direction so that the driver's doors were side by side. Mancuso got out and waited for Dale to open his window. "Mr. Luciano wants to speak to you," he said.

"I don't have time for this," said Dale.

Mancuso ignored him and turned to open the rear passenger door on the driver's side and hold it open. Again, Dale hesitated and tried to think of a better choice than climbing into the car with Tony Luciano.

OK, let's get this over with. He got out of his car. He went to the back seat of the limo and saw Tony sitting there, grey suit and red tie this time, same brown shoes, no friendly greeting. "Have a seat, Hunter," he said.

Dale got in and turned to face him. Mancuso closed the door behind Dale and got back into the driver's seat, pulling his door shut.

Shit. I hope we're not going for a drive. Just another friendly chat, I was thinking. Mancuso kept his eyes forward and did not start the car.

Luciano spoke. "I thought we had an understanding, Hunter, but you seem to insist on going places where you don't belong. I thought you were a smart businessman and knew how to avoid risks. And yet, you still wanna get involved in this mess with Bobbie Brydon. Didn't I warn you to back off?"

"Yes, I got that message," said Dale. "I did back off. I left it to the police to do their job. I'm not sticking my nose in anymore."

"That's not what I hear. First, you accuse Donna Brydon of being involved in the death of her husband, then the cops are thinking it might be a murder instead of a suicide and you send them in my direction. So yesterday the cops are back in my face asking more stupid questions. What the hell are you doing?"

His raised voice grabbed Dale's attention and he forced back the rising fear in his belly. "I'm just defending myself, dammit. I'm trying to get some answers too, so the police stop accusing me of Brydon's murder. I didn't kill him, but they still have me on their list of suspects."

"Well now they're wasting *my* time on this bullshit. You and the cops need to listen to Lisa. There was no murder here. And I sure as hell had nothing to do with it. You need to back off like I told you already and take the cops with you."

"The cops don't take directions from me. I have no control over who they investigate and what they decide."

Luciano looked unconvinced. "Listen, Hunter, there are a lot of possibilities here and it's up to you to get this under control. You seem to be the joker in the deck who keeps fucking it up. I'm giving you one last chance to fix it up, instead. You have two choices." He waited for Dale's full attention. "Either you help convince them it was suicide and stop looking for a murderer, or you confess to killing him yourself."

"Those are not good choices."

"That's all I've got for you. Make it happen, Hunter. I don't want the police calling on me again."

"I'll do what I can. But they're going to make their own choices. You and me both want the same thing. We want them to end this, suicide or not, and leave us alone. We can agree on that can't we?"

Luciano gave him a hard look without showing any agreement. "I hope you get it done this time," he said. "This is our last meeting. You won't see me again. Don't make me send somebody else to look after you. You need to think about how badly this could go for you. You need to think about your family. We know where you live."

Luciano paused and watched Dale thinking about it. He added, "Don't worry about the cops, worry about me."

He gave Dale another long look while that message settled in. He tipped his head at the door. "Now get outta here."

Dale got out and went back into his car.

Mancuso pulled away and Dale's thoughts danced between the threats he's heard and the choices he had to make to protect himself and his family. He wondered about his next move. Should he even go to another meeting with Hélène Bourassa and Claude Samson?

He started his car, slowly merged with the traffic again on St. Charles Boulevard, and headed to the office.

36.

Back at the office, Dale had long forgotten his relaxing weekend reconnecting with his wife and kids. It had been great to celebrate Susan's return to good health and see the kids noticeably relieved that she was back to her old self again, but it was another Monday morning and Dale was back into the pressing issues for his business.

He'd already had a good meeting with Theresa Leblanc and he was confirming the conclusions with Monique Chevrier. "You can tell Paul Macrae that we don't need to reply to the letter from Theresa's attorney," he said. "We had a good meeting this morning and she's satisfied now with the job I set up for her with Jean-Guy Brassard at Phoenix Systems. It's essentially a promotion for her. Something we didn't have for her here. It will be better pay, more challenging, and a perfect fit for her technical skills and personality as a customer service rep with Phoenix. I managed to explain it would be better for her career and look better on her resumé than a lawsuit against a previous employer. That's never very appealing for the next potential employer."

"That's better for everybody," said Monique. "I'm sure Theresa knew that your recommendation was sincere and not just a polite way of letting her go. Well done, Dale."

She smiled and then added, "However, your next

challenge is waiting at reception. That young detective, Pat Carney, wants to see you for a few minutes, he says. Marie wanted me to ask what you wanted her to tell him. She already said she wasn't sure you were available, but he doesn't look like he's leaving anytime soon."

"I thought these guys were done with me. Brydon is buried and the file is closed I thought. Anyway, I'll have to see what he wants and send him away myself, I guess. Send him in. Thanks, Monique"

What the hell? First Luciano, now the cops?

A few seconds later, Detective Pat Carney strode briskly down the hall and into Dale's office. "Hello, Hunter," he said, "thanks for making some time in your busy day for me." He pulled a chair back from Dale's desk and settled his lean muscled frame into it. "I won't be long." He looked like he was prepared to stay as long as he wanted.

Dale took a look at him before replying. Each time they met, he noticed that Carney was constantly moving and shifting his body from one position to another, arms crossed then elbows on the arms of the chair, hands clasped together, then rubbing his chin. His eyes, however, remained constantly focused on Dale and his response to every question.

Dale asked the first question. "Why are you here, detective? I thought you were done with me. You're not still investigating Bobbie Brydon's death, are you? I've got nothing new for you on that subject."

"Still a few loose ends and I do have some questions for

you," said Carney. "I'm interested in your history with the Mafia in Montreal, especially the Luciano family."

"I have no history with the Luciano family."

"I heard you've had several encounters with their criminal activities in the past. Never an active mobster, I'm told, but still you got involved in the protection racket, loan sharking, money laundering, maybe more. So, I have questions about your current connections to organized crime."

"You make it sound like I'm a dangerous criminal myself," said Dale, shaking his head. "I was forced to do some things I never wanted to do to protect my business and my family, and that was with other gangsters, never the Lucianos. I didn't even know Donna Brydon was related to the Lucianos until after Bobbie's death."

He scowled at Carney. "You really are nuts if you think I was ever part of the Mob. I didn't even know what a mobster was until I arrived here from a small town in Western Canada and started reading the newspapers in Montreal."

Carney shrugged. "But once you got involved, how do we know you never joined the dark side? Maybe you learned the money is better in organized crime than it is in the computer business. Easy money, if you do business with those guys."

"It's never easy and not the way I ever want to make money."

"But you did do business with them. How do we know

you're not doing business with them again?"

"The only way I ever did business with them is under threats of violence or destruction of my business. Threats on my life and my family, murder and kidnapping. Once they blew up my car in the driveway at home. I was never a willing partner in their crimes and always cooperated with the police to end it."

"So, what are they threatening you with this time? What are you doing for them now? What did you do for them to get rid of Bobbie Brydon?"

Dale gritted his teeth and took a long breath before exhaling slowly.

"I'm thinking I should just tell you to fuck off and leave me alone. Maybe we should schedule another meeting in your little interview room downtown, and I'll bring my lawyer along next time." He looked at Carney staring back at him without reply.

Dale continued, "But let me be more polite and helpful than that and give you a chance to show that you're smarter than you seem. Or prove that you're not."

He leaned forward and placed his elbows on the desk, hands clasped in front of him. "After Bobbie Brydon's death, since I was a so-called family friend, I was directed by Hélène Bourassa and your colleague, Detective Claude Samson, to push Donna Brydon for more information on her connections with the Luciano family. Then, as expected, we got a reaction from her cousin, Tony Luciano. He told me, essentially, to butt out and stop suggesting any involvement of Donna, or him, in Bobbie Brydon's death. Unfortunately for me, you intelligent detectives decided to keep pushing his buttons, and he decided *I* was the problem. So, earlier this morning he warned me again in stronger language."

Dale put his hands on the desk and drummed his fingers. "He and his strongman intercepted me on the way to work and pulled me over for a little word of advice."

He added, "As an expert in organised crime, I'm sure you know what 'remove you ourselves,' really means for me, if I don't butt out. Today he reminded me that my family was also at risk, and more from him than from any investigation by the police. However, he did have a solution for me to solve all those problems. He gave me two choices. He wants me to persuade you that Brydon committed suicide, or confess that I killed him myself."

Carney relaxed his gaze and almost smiled. "So, which did you decide to do?"

"I'm not confessing to something I never did, so I'm hoping you'll eventually accept the suicide explanation and leave me and Tony Luciano alone. Your visit here today is not a good sign you're going to do that."

Carney put both hands down on the arms of his chair and lifted himself up to stand in front of Dale. His intense gaze returned as he said, "Actually, I think you've made some progress answering my questions. I appreciate your honesty. Was that the whole truth or do you have more to tell me?"

"That's all I've got. I don't want any more visits from you or Tony Luciano. Leave me alone so I can get back to business. I've got better things to do, and so do you, I'm sure."

Carney wasn't ready to concede on that point, but he said, "Thanks again for your time." He turned and left the office. On the way back downtown to Station 21, he wondered what he would report to his partner, Claude Samson. In their attempts to avoid implicating Donna or Lisa Brydon in their suspicions of Tony Luciano, had they pushed him instead to threaten Dale Hunter? Was Hunter in danger again as an innocent bystander?

Or was he just a good liar?

37.

Detectives Hélène Bourassa and Claude Samson were sitting in their unmarked blue Chrysler sedan outside the home of Bobbie Brydon in Westmount. They were on the other side of the street facing the house so they could both see it through the windshield.

"Looks pretty quiet," said Claude. "This time of the morning, she's probably not even up yet. How are we going to explain us dropping in unannounced for her wake-up call? She's gonna be even more of an angry bitch this time around."

Hélène gave him a sideways glance. "You're going to have to turn on the charm again, Claude. We don't have a good reason to be here. I just want to follow up and let her know we have a strong denial from Tony Luciano after we asked him if he might have *misunderstood,* like she suggested."

"But we never pushed Luciano very hard that it was her suggestion. We know he's not going to be happy with anybody who's sending us in his direction. We tried to keep him in the dark where our information was coming from." He watched the front door and mumbled to himself. "But he probably knows the dumb bitch talks too much."

Hélène raised an eyebrow and looked at Claude. "Maybe, but he also knows who else we're talking to about

Brydon's possible homicide. Maybe he doesn't know about Vinnie Mancuso's interest in Donna. According to Frank, he's more fond of her than you are, Claude."

Claude shook his head. "Hard to figure. Definitely not my kinda woman." Claude and his wife had separated years ago, and he was not involved with anyone else as far as Hélène knew. A lonesome, dedicated cop with no one to share his life with except the other detectives he worked with.

Hélène looked back toward the front door of Brydon's mansion and still saw no sign of anyone up and about in the house. She said, "I'd also like to know if Donna encouraged Vinnie in his fantasies for her. Maybe she asked *him* for help in getting rid of her husband in return for a little extra attention."

"Jesus, I'd be running for cover if she offered me any extra attention." Claude shuddered. "Anyway, let's go make her day and get her riled up again. She does enjoy my attention. Gives her somebody new to curse at."

Hélène smiled at Claude's characterization of his meetings with Donna Brydon. She was thinking they had more in common than Claude would admit. Both were tough, cynical, and quick to bark at anyone who crossed them, especially if they thought they were being unreasonable or uncooperative.

The two detectives got out of their car and walked across the street and up the driveway. Hélène nodded at the realtor's sign, For Sale – *A Vendre,* at the sidewalk. "I guess she's looking to cash out on the house now, too. It's all working out very well for Mrs. Brydon."

At the front door, after three long rings of the doorbell, there was no response. "Must be sleeping-in with one of the boyfriends," said Claude. He moved up to the side window by the door and shielded his eyes to peer in.

"Oh, shit! She's lying in the hallway. It looks like she's been shot!"

He stepped back and let Hélène move forward to look for herself.

She looked in through the curtains and saw Donna Brydon lying sprawled on her back in the hallway, wounds in her chest bleeding out through her white blouse onto the carpet.

Hélène stood back and said, "Call it in and ask for help."

Claude started down the steps to go back and use the car radio as Hélène reached into her side pocket and pulled out a pair of blue surgical gloves before trying the door handle. It was unlocked.

"Wait a minute," she called out, "come in with me first. We'll check this out before we call it in."

Claude turned back and pulled his gun out of the holster to follow her into the hallway and stand back in the doorway with his gun, ready to defend her. He glanced back over his shoulder and saw nobody watching or leaving the scene. He listened for any other signs of life in the house and watched Hélène kneel beside the still body on the floor.

She checked for a pulse at the neck. The cold skin

confirmed there were no signs of life left in Donna Brydon.

"Keep those gloves on," said Claude. "There's a lot of blood here and she had a lot of sex with strangers. That means a high risk of AIDS. You don't want to take any chances."

"Close the door and lock it," said Hélène. "Let's check out the rest of the house before we call it in."

The rest of the house was empty with no other signs of violence. Hélène stayed to examine the scene as Claude went out to the car to call in a report and ask for assistance. She took a pad out of her vest pocket and started making notes. Three fatal shots to the chest and no signs of resistance or struggle.

An inspection down the hallway led her to discover that two of the large-calibre bullets had gone through the body and lodged in the wall. One of them had passed through a framed oil-painting of bright-coloured modern art. It was still hanging straight and Hélène lifted it gently to confirm the bullet hole behind with a slug buried deep in the plaster. The third shot must have come after Donna fell to the floor and might be buried in the floorboards beneath her. Hélène was not planning to move the body and find out. The crime scene crew could do that. She scanned the area and noted there were no shell casings nearby. Definitely not a suicide this time and no amateur would be so thorough and efficient, killing her and leaving no evidence. She wrote at the end of her notes: *Professional hit?*

When the investigating team arrived and settled into

their work, Hélène went out front to look for Claude. He was chatting to the uniformed officer who had left his car in the driveway with the lights flashing. "He can turn the flashers off, there's no emergency here now," she said. "You and I have more work to do, Claude."

She put her notepad back in the vest pocket of her suit jacket and gestured toward their vehicle. "We're going to have to visit Lisa and tell her what happened here. That's going to be hard."

Claude nodded. "Yeah. Poor kid. At least she didn't walk in on this one herself."

At Lisa's apartment, the second time for Hélène and the first visit for Claude, it was a much more agitated conversation. Lisa was distraught.

She screamed at Hélène, "This is your fault!" She stepped forward and slammed her hands on Hélène's shoulders, pushing her backwards. "You never should have told Uncle Tony. He warned her not to say anything to you. Now he had to shut her up!"

Hélène reached up and held Lisa's wrists to hold her away from her. "We never told Tony anything about your mother or what she said to us. He maybe assumed we heard something from her, but we never told him."

"But she's dead! Shot in her own house." Lisa pulled herself away and fell into a heap in the armchair in her living room. "My god, what's happening? First my dad, now my mom." She collapsed in heavy sobs. "Just leave me alone. You only make matters worse. Go away!"

"Is there anyone we can call for you, Lisa? You shouldn't be alone," said Hélène.

"I can call for myself. Just go."

Lisa turned away in tears and hugged herself to keep her distress under control. Hélène and Claude exchanged sympathetic looks, then turned and quietly left the apartment.

38.

Three days later in the open office area at Station 21, Claude was putting his phone down to look up at Hélène standing beside his desk waiting to speak to him. "I just got a tip on Donna Brydon's murder," she said. "Somebody knows something he thinks we should know. You want to come with me and hear the whole story?"

Claude looked confused. "What? Who?"

"It might be a complete waste of time," said Hélène, "but remember your friend, the elegant Mr. Richardson, who thought we wanted him to manage our pension funds? He just called to say he has some information that might be helpful to us. He said he just heard of Donna Brydon's murder and thought he should be a responsible citizen and speak to us about it. Strictly confidential of course, doesn't want his name mentioned anywhere."

"Yeah, right," said Claude. "Maybe he wants to pitch us on managing our own fortunes."

"Not worth his time, remember?"

"Oh, yeah. But he really didn't seem very interested in being helpful last time, either."

"Maybe something's changed. Let's go see him and find out what he knows that he wants to share with us now."

Back in Richardson's office, they sat in the same uncomfortable easy chairs opposite Richardson, who looked a little less comfortable himself this time. He tried to remain emotionless but appeared to be choosing his words very carefully as he explained why he had called.

"I think maybe a client of mine may have had a score to settle with Donna Brydon." He paused to confirm he had their attention.

"About six months ago, I introduced him, uh … to Donna's network. He wanted to meet one of her girls. I explained who Donna was and her family connection to the Lucianos. That's when he became very interested in meeting Donna herself. He got quite excited about it and said something about how he'd been fucked by the Lucianos, and he would really love to uh, … fuck 'em back. Sorry, but those were the words he used."

He shifted in his chair before continuing. "He was very interested in me introducing him to her. He didn't intend to pay an escort for her services though, he wanted to seduce Donna and then fuck her. Uh, … in every sense of the word." He poured himself a glass of water from the crystal carafe on the coffee table and took a long drink, collecting his thoughts before continuing. Hélène and Claude sat quietly waiting for more.

"My client apparently got what he wanted from Donna, sex for revenge or whatever it was, and then it came to a very ugly end. They really got into it and exchanged threats of violence. Both are very volatile personalities and quick to explode. I tried to intervene and calm them down when they complained to me about each other. As if I had introduced them to enjoy the spectacle." He was shaking his head at the thought. "I tried to calm them down, but maybe he still hated her enough to pull a gun on her. I don't know."

Hélène looked sceptical. "That's all you've got for us? It's a pretty serious accusation with not much to go on."

Claude added, "She had a lot of boyfriends, he's probably not the only one who wanted to kill her. Do you have a name for us on this guy?"

Robinson looked from Claude to Hélène and handed her a printed page, no letterhead, with a name and contact details on it. He said, "You need to keep this information confidential. I'm not protected by lawyer-client privilege, so I have to tell you what I know, but I can't afford to have any client think I'm not keeping their secrets. The only reason I'm giving you this is to avoid any subsequent accusations of obstruction of justice. I was very co-operative, I think you'll agree, during your last inquiries about Donna Brydon and I don't want you to ever come back with suggestions I was withholding any information that might have helped you in your investigations of her husband's death or her own." He paused and raised his eyebrows, waiting for acknowledgement from Hélène.

She ignored him and showed the name to Claude.

Claude looked startled and said, "Daniel Kristopoulos? The restaurant guy? I guess he has enough money to make it worth your while to look after him." Claude tossed

Richardson's own words back at him. "As you said, good customer service is important. Whatever he wanted."

"I do remember him having some problems, and a couple of his restaurants were blown up during the pizza wars with organized crime," said Hélène. "His company, Kristo Foods, is also big in the supply of olive oil, pasta, and cheese, so that's probably where he got into conflict with the Lucianos. There's a lot of money to fight over in the pizza business, apparently."

"I don't know any more than what I've told you," said Richardson. "It's up to you to decide what to investigate from here if anything. Let's leave it at that."

Hélène nodded, folded the single sheet, and placed it inside the front of her notebook.

Claude looked like he was considering a more aggressive line of questioning, but he saw Hélène putting her notebook away and said, "Fine, thanks, we'll look into it. We appreciate you being such a responsible citizen and sharing confidential client information, Mr. Richardson. It should be no problem for you." He rose from his chair and added, "Unless, of course, we have to look into your aiding and abetting Donna Brydon in her sex trafficking business. Sorry, matchmaking. I know that's what you prefer to call it."

Richardson gave Claude a blank stare, then nodded to Hélène and returned to his desk. Claude smirked to himself as they left the office to return to Station 21.

39.

The island of Montreal is comprised of twenty-nine separate municipalities that make up Greater Montreal. In the northeast is the largely Italian community of Saint Leonard. Away from the shopping centres and strip malls, the residential neighbourhoods and the city parks, is a sprawling light-industrial section where the offices and warehouses of Kristo Foods were located. Detectives Claude Samson and Pat Carney had arrived unannounced at the spacious reception area on the mezzanine floor to introduce themselves and ask for Mr. Daniel Kristopoulos.

They were advised by the receptionist, "I'm sorry he's not available. You have to phone ahead to make an appointment with Mr. Kristopoulos."

"Yeah, yeah," said Claude. "Just tell him we're a coupla homicide detectives from Montreal looking for his help with some information we need. We don't have a warrant and he doesn't need his lawyer. We can go that route if he insists, but we just want ten minutes of his time for a coupla questions."

The receptionist looked a little more interested. "Just a moment, please," she said, removing her headset, and went down the hall out of sight.

Claude and Pat stepped back and Claude found a large comfortable armchair to sit in and wait. He pulled out his notepad and started writing on a fresh page. Pat remained standing and prowled the reception area looking at the framed photos and product ads mounted on the walls alongside the awards and trophies placed in a large glass case. He quickly gained the impression that Kristo Foods was a global corporation with a wide range of products for restaurants and grocery stores.

The receptionist returned, watching Carney's meandering before speaking to them. "If it's only ten minutes he'll be here shortly. You can wait for him in the conference room."

She turned to lead the way down another corridor and opened the door to a small conference room with a row of windows looking out over the front parking lot. Claude took a seat on the far side of the oval-shaped dark hardwood table and Pat continued his tour of the photos and mementos that were also mounted on the walls of the conference room. He took his time to complete the tour and then sat down beside Claude, placed his notepad on the table, pushed his chair back, and stretched out with one foot on his knee, still without any sign of Kristopoulos. He looked at Claude and asked, "How long do you think he'll make us wait?"

"He's a very important, busy guy," said Claude. "He wants us to know that. So he'll be at least thirty minutes."

It took longer than that before the door opened and Daniel Kristopoulos walked in. He was a heavy-set handsome man, with a deep-tanned face and a head of long wavy grey hair, dressed in a button-down white shirt with his sleeves rolled up, light-brown cotton slacks and bare feet in tasseled red-suede loafers. He pulled up a chair opposite the two detectives and sat forward with his hands on the table. "I have two minutes, gentleman. What can I do for you?"

"Fine," said Claude. "We'll be quick." He leaned over his notepad and flipped it open at the page where he had started by noting the date, time and place. He placed his pen on the page and asked, "I understand you know Mrs. Donna Brydon of Westmount."

"Yes." Kristopoulos waited for the next question.

"Do you know she was murdered in her home last week?"

"Yes."

"Do you know anything about her murder that we should be aware of?"

"I didn't do it." He paused and looked from Claude to Pat Carney.

Back to Claude, "Any more questions?"

Claude asked, "Did you also know she was related to Tony Luciano?"

"Yes."

"We understand that you had some prior business conflict with Tony Luciano."

His complexion grew darker. "No comment."

"We also understand that you were in an intimate relationship with Donna Brydon that ended badly. There was apparently some incident with an altercation and mutual threats of violence."

Kristopoulos was very still. His jaw line tightened before he hissed, "That sleazy son-of-a-bitch Richardson sent you here."

Carney flinched, not imperceptibly. Claude took a moment to respond. "Who's Richardson? Why would he do that?"

Kristopoulos nodded at Carney and said to Claude, "As I'm sure you know, Richardson introduced me to Donna Brydon and it turned out to be a disaster. He probably told you that. But he probably didn't tell you that it didn't end well for him either. I moved all my money to another manager and decided to sue him for failing in his duties to look after my money as promised. He's been fighting back with his own threats to disclose confidential information about my finances that would do some damage to me. It's just a useless pissing contest, of course, neither of us want any outsiders looking too close at our financial affairs."

Kristopoulos sat back and tapped his fingers on the table.

"But this goes too far," he said. "Sending you after me on a wild goose chase and wasting your time and mine. You can tell him we now have a new score to settle and the next move is mine." He forced a phony smile, then rolled his chair back to get up and leave.

"One more question," said Claude. "Where were you on the evening of August seventeenth?"

"Really?" said Kristopoulos. "We're not done yet?"

"We have to finish what we started," said Claude.

"OK, that's the last question, then we're done." He stood before answering. "For your information, I was in Greece the last three weeks and just got back on the weekend. On the seventeenth, I was probably at my home in Piraeus."

"You have the travel receipts to show us?"

"Of course. I'll have my secretary bring copies to you. Good day, gentlemen." He turned and left, closing the door behind him.

Pat Carney looked at his watch. "That took about seven minutes, after waiting here for forty-five minutes. How long do you think he'll make us wait this time?"

"Patience, Pat, patience. Now he's proved who's in charge he'll be quick to get us out of here. We're done. I think we can forget him as a suspect."

Less than ten minutes later, a woman arrived to show them the original flight itinerary to Greece and back to Montreal with the tickets and boarding passes, then she slid photocopies of each across the table for them to take away.

"Thanks," said Claude, "we'll take the originals. You can keep the photocopies."

She nodded, pulled back the photocopies and put the originals in a folder which she pushed toward them and left the room.

Pat said, "Another test?"

Claude smiled. "I think he's done this before."

40.

Later, back at Station 21, Claude pushed himself up out of his chair and away from his desk to walk out of the open office area with its busy detectives engaged in animated conversations, some standing and leaning over the few fabric-covered, entirely useless, privacy partitions. Some were focused on their phone calls, trying to hear over the surrounding chatter, and others were browsing the array of paperwork, notes and files in front of them. They were busy; not necessarily making the progress they wanted in solving crimes, but sharing their challenges with other officers sometimes eased the frustrations.

Claude shuffled down the hall leading to the private office of Detective-Sergeant Hélène Bourassa and leaned in through the door. Hélène looked up and covered the mouthpiece of the phone she was on. She raised her eyebrows in query to Claude.

"Sorry to interrupt, Hélène, but I have some news for you," he said.

Hélène held up one figure for him to stand by for a second. She uncovered the phone to say, "Sorry Maxine, but I'm going to have to leave it at that for now, I've got an annoying detective interrupting me here at the moment. I'll call you back if I think of anything else on your case." She flipped the phone cord off her desk and down along the wall before placing the receiver back in its cradle and looking up at Claude.

He said, "I know you were disappointed we wasted our time on Richardson's little vendetta against Daniel Kristopoulos and we might actually have some good news for a change."

"We could use a break on that friggin' case," she said. "What've you got?"

Claude replied, "I just heard from Léo. He has a report ready for us and I think you should come with me to see what he's got."

"Léo who?" she asked.

"Léo Théberge, the forensics lab manager downstairs. I asked him to check again for fingerprints or DNA in the evidence from Bobbie Brydon's death and from his wife's murder, too. He tells me he has something interesting for us."

"I thought we already checked for prints and DNA."

"We did, but I asked him to take a closer look at the shell casings. We didn't do that the first time around."

"But we checked the gun from Bobbie's crime scene, and at Donna Brydon's we didn't have a gun or see any shell casings left behind in the house anyway. That's what indicated a professional hit, I thought."

"Well, professional or not, the investigators found one shell under Donna's body when they lifted it off the floor."

"And Théberge found something that may tie the two deaths together?"

"He didn't go that far. Just said we'd find it *interesting*."

They went downstairs together to the cold, sterile basement where the small lab and a morgue for holding bodies and processing crime victims were located. Outside Théberge's small office there were two technicians in white lab coats sitting at countertops in the lab peering into microscopes and moving samples in and out of the slide tray.

On the way by, Claude said, "Soon they'll be solving all these cases in the lab. No need for grinding away at detective work anymore. Just find the forensic evidence and it's all over. Your Honour, we've got all the proof we need."

"Don't get too excited, Claude, it's never going to be that easy."

They sat in front of Théberge in the hard, straight-backed visitor chairs in his office. Théberge also wore a white lab coat with a badge and name tag clipped to the pocket. He was a lean, long-limbed, young man with unruly brown hair and oval-shaped, wire-rimmed glasses low on his nose. He leaned his bony elbows on the desk and looked at them with bright enthusiasm. Hélène found herself thinking of John Lennon singing about giving peace a chance.

Théberge looked pleased to be in the spotlight with two detectives waiting to hear the results of his analysis. He was enjoying increasing levels of respect and credibility from these skeptical, old-fashioned detectives as they started to appreciate how modern forensic science could give them new answers in their investigations and give prosecuting attorneys important evidence to put before the judge and jury. Théberge did not intend to be brief and to the point, although he expected the young lady detective, who was clearly the senior officer, would probably run out of patience if he didn't share his conclusions fairly quickly.

He had two file folders on his desk lying closed, side by side. He placed a palm on each one and said, "As requested, we took a more thorough look at the evidence in both these cases."

He patted the two files on the desk in front of him, right hand then left, "First was Mr. Bobbie Brydon, killed by a single shot from a Glock 17 semi-automatic handgun. Then we have Mrs. Donna Brydon, who was killed by three shots from a large calibre revolver, probably a Colt .357 Magnum."

He nodded to Claude and said, "Detective Samson had the brilliant idea of taking a closer look at the shell casings in particular, and that did, in fact, give us new evidence that I think you'll find interesting." No harm in a little flattery to keep his audience's attention.

He continued. "We examined the spent casing found beside the body of Bobbie Brydon and the five remaining bullets in the cartridge. From the scene of Donna Brydon's murder we do not have a gun to analyze, but we did find two slugs buried in the wall and one more in the floor." He paused and flicked his eyebrows with a quick smile at his audience. "Plus, one shell casing that was found under her body. We tied that shell to the bullet that went through her chest and lodged in the wall behind a painting it had passed through."

The two detectives acknowledged his exposition and nodded quickly to speed him along.

Théberge said, "We did not find any DNA which might have been more definitive, but we did find fingerprints on all the shell casings. As you know, we have access to an extensive database of all the fingerprints of suspects processed in any of the Montreal precincts and, of course, we've added the prints of all the witnesses and persons of interest in these two cases. Our software is regularly updated and it's exceptionally efficient at rapidly scanning the database and identifying any fingerprints on file that match."

He tapped on the two file folders. "On the shell casings from these two crime scenes, we have distinct fingerprints identified with over ninety-nine-point-nine percent certainty, but they are *not* the same fingerprints at both crime scenes."

Claude frowned. "You mean nothing ties the two cases together?"

Hélène said, "What were the two matches then?"

"Yes, very interesting," said Théberge with a self-satisfied smile, pushing his glasses up his nose to look up from the paperwork to his audience.

"The two *victims* were related, but the two people whose fingerprints we found are not." He paused for dramatic effect, before delivering the punch line.

"On the single bullet found under Donna Brydon's body we discovered the prints of a known criminal with

Mafia connections, Mr. Vincenzo Mancuso. What was more surprising to me, but maybe not to you, was that the fingerprints on the shell casing of the bullet that killed Mr. Bobby Brydon and on those remaining in the gun that was used to kill him were the prints of his daughter, Miss Lisa Brydon."

"Holy shit," said Claude. He looked quickly from Théberge to Hélène.

She sat back and gazed at the two files on Théberge's desk. "Now that is interesting," she said.

She looked back at Claude. "Now we finally have some evidence to work with. It doesn't give us all the answers yet, but we definitely have some tougher questions to ask. Let's set up our next interviews with Vinnie Mancuso and Lisa Brydon. Mancuso first."

"Thank you, Léo," said Claude. "You're right, that was brilliant." He looked hopefully at Hélène to see if she was giving him any credit. They went back upstairs and Claude eased his bulk into the uncomfortable visitor chair again in Hélène's office. They both had questions running through their heads.

Who killed Donna Brydon? Was it the same person who killed Bobbie? Why would Vinnie kill Donna if he cared so much about her? Could Tony have persuaded him to do it?

Did Lisa kill her own father or did somebody use her gun? Did Bobbie use it on himself?

Claude spoke first. "I know we've linked Vinnie to the gun that killed Donna Brydon, but it still makes no sense.

Even if Tony Luciano wanted her dead for some reason, the Mafia don't usually kill their own family members, especially not the women. Maybe somebody took the gun away from her and killed her with it for some other reason altogether …" He ran out of steam and couldn't bring that train of thought to a logical conclusion.

Hélène was shaking her head. "I don't know either. And what about Lisa's gun? You think she used it on her dad?"

"No way," exclaimed Claude. "That poor, fragile little lady is in bad shape ever since she found him dead like that. She's gonna collapse entirely if we start pushing her any harder. You want to treat *her* as a suspect now?"

He sat back and scratched his head, scowling as he thought a little more about it. "I can't explain it, though. Her gun, her bullets. Did her dad use it on himself or did somebody else pull the trigger?"

Hélène said, "Yeah, tough questions. I'm not looking forward to asking them, but we need to bring her in. I don't think we're going to be friends again after that."

Claude smiled. "You didn't take this job to make friends, Hélène. But I think you're right. You won't have any friends left in the Luciano family, that's for sure."

41.

Hélène and Claude were parked the next day in one of the visitor spaces facing the fence along the sidewalk in front of Agile Construction. They got out of the car together and strode toward the front doors. Hélène scanned the surrounding streets of five to eight-story brick buildings in the historic Lachine Canal area southwest of downtown which had been the industrial heart of Canada when the canal was built in the mid-nineteenth century. She glanced at signs of the modern economy still doing business in the area, then lifted her hand in a signal to the blue and white patrol car parked down the street.

Claude asked her, "Are you sure Mancuso is here?"

"Yes," she said, "I've had surveillance here all morning and they confirmed both Tony and Vinnie are here now. I want to see them together and get their reaction to each other as well as the new evidence we have."

A few minutes later, they were in the elegant, spacious office of Tony Luciano. It was not Hélène's first visit, or Claude's. The office had dark wood-panelled walls, soft leather furniture and subdued lighting with a few spotlights on the classical paintings of Italian scenes. They were standing in front of Tony's desk as he leaned back in his chair and said, "So, to what do I owe the pleasure of a meeting with the lovely and charming Detective Hélène

Bourassa today?"

Hélène declined to correct him on her rank and said, "Thank you for making time for us, but we'd also like to see Mr. Vincenzo Mancuso here today. I understand he's in the building."

"I see," said Tony with a smug grin. "I'm sure you know he's in the building. So, you brought along your tough guy, Detective Samson, to meet with my tough guy, Vinnie Mancuso." His eyes slowly scanned the two detectives. "You seem so sweet and gentle yourself, detective, but I have a feeling you can be pretty tough too."

He squeezed his lips together in a phony smile and reached for his phone on the desk. He gestured to a large conference table on the far side of his office. "Have a seat and I'll call for Vinnie to join us. I hope you're going to make it fast, though. We're very busy. You know it's a short construction season in Montreal."

"We plan to be brief," said Hélène. "It won't take long, if you're willing to co-operate."

Tony Luciano didn't smile again. Hélène and Claude went to sit at the large conference table with its four high-backed armchairs along each side and one more at each end. They sat together on one side while Tony called for Vinnie Mancuso to join them.

When Vinnie arrived a few minutes later, he sat opposite the two detectives and Luciano sat at the end closest to his desk at the head of the table. It was the biggest armchair.

Hélène opened the conversation. Looking at them

both, she said, "We have talked to you before and you're both aware of our investigation into the deaths of Bobbie Brydon and his wife, Donna Brydon."

All three men at the table remained expressionless, watching and waiting for her to continue. She looked at Tony and Vinnie in turn, then said, "We now have new evidence from the forensic investigators that proves ownership of the guns used at each crime scene. The first, used in the death of Bobbie Brydon, was a Glock that appears to have belonged to his daughter, Lisa Brydon. And the second, used in the killing of Donna Brydon, was a Colt .357 belonging to you, Vinnie."

She saw Vinnie look genuinely surprised, and Tony, equally surprised, was suddenly scowling at him.

"Don't say anything," said Tony. "They're bluffing. If they really had solid evidence they would be taking you downtown and I'd have our lawyer there for you before you talk to them."

Vinnie was nodding and rocking back and forth in his chair. He looked at Hélène and said, "I think I can save you the trouble and explain both guns."

Now it was Claude who looked intrigued with Vinnie's statement. He leaned forward but resisted the temptation to pick up his notepad and pen.

Hélène said, "Alright, let's hear it."

"Careful, Vinnie," said Tony, "she'll use whatever she gets from you and it may not be good for either of us."

Vinnie's eyes flicked to Tony, then he looked at Hélène

with a confident smile. "I'm sure her mother told her the same as mine told me, you never go wrong telling the truth."

"That's not what my mother told me," said Tony. "It's always better to keep your mouth shut to stay out of trouble. Everybody has a different version of what's the truth."

Vinnie looked at Hélène. "Here's my version," he said. "It'll be the same even if Tony's lawyer's listening. You'll have to decide for yourself what you're gonna believe."

Hélène nodded at him as he continued. "I gave them those guns. Actually, I gave both guns to Lisa, one for her mother. They wanted to be safe in this dangerous world we live in, especially with all the shit going on around Tony and the threats he was up against from, uh … enemies of the family."

"Did you load both guns yourself," asked Hélène.

"Yes, I loaded both guns and gave them each a box of shells. I offered to show them how to use them safely, but I was told Donna didn't need any lessons. Lisa was kind of nervous to start with, but she got pretty good with the Glock after some practice at the range."

Hélène asked. "How do you explain that your fingerprints were not on that gun and not on the spent shell casing beside Bobbie Brydon's body or on any of the shells remaining in the gun cartridge."

Vinnie shrugged. "Lisa used that gun a lot at the range and would have reloaded it herself. I know she bought another box of shells."

"Where'd you get the two guns," asked Claude. "From

Tony?"

That got a dark scowl from the end of the table.

"Hell no," said Vinnie, sneering at Samson. "I don't remember where the guns came from. I had them in a safe at home. Maybe took 'em away from some asshole who wanted to use 'em on us."

Tony said, "That's enough, Vinnie. We're done here." He turned his glare on Claude and Hélène. "We're not answering any more questions."

"Fine," said Hélène, "Let's go downtown and we'll get your statement in writing and then get a warrant to go to your place and open that safe you're talking about."

"Goddamn it, my mother was right," said Tony.

Vinnie glared at her, "You seem so reasonable, but you're pretty sneaky, alright. That's the last time I'm co-operating. Get your goddamn search warrant."

"Well, you'll still have to come with us to the station, Vinnie," said Hélène. "You're now under arrest for the murder of Donna Brydon and we can't give you the opportunity to go clean out the safe."

She stood and gestured to Claude. "Go ahead," she said.

Claude got out of his chair to put the cuffs on Vinnie who stood up with a snarl of foul language as he turned to Claude and held his hands out.

"Thanks for your help, Tony," said Hélène. "We'll let you know if we have any more questions." Tony gave her another dark look, but refrained from unleashing an impolite farewell.

42.

Hélène decided not to call on Lisa with another detective, especially not Claude Samson, who seemed to have trouble thinking of Lisa as a potential suspect in the deaths of her parents. Hélène's big sister approach had made Lisa more receptive the last time, so she attempted that attitude again. It didn't go so well this time.

As soon as Hélène explained they had found Lisa's fingerprints on the gun used to kill her father, she collapsed in a flood of tears and heart-rending sobs. As Claude had expected. Between sobs, Lisa's words came out in emotional bursts.

"Oh, my God! ... I know. It was my gun ... I gave it to him! He wanted it for protection, I thought. He said he was worried about Uncle Tony ... I never thought he'd kill himself with it!"

She caught her breath and slowed the sobs to a quiet whimper. "I couldn't tell you it was my gun ... you started talking about murder! I knew it was suicide. He used the gun I gave him!"

Hélène sat quietly, waiting for Lisa to calm herself.

The tears stopped and Lisa took a few more deep breaths. "I'm so sorry, Hélène, I know I should have told you sooner about the gun. But ... but I was hoping you would figure it out yourself ... if it was suicide or murder.

You didn't need to know it was my gun. Oh, my God, I feel so guilty!" She shuddered. "If it was murder, somebody killed him with my gun!"

Hélène looked at her closely and said, "You're right, Lisa. It would have been better to tell us sooner. I know it was a difficult time for you and it was hard to know the right thing to do."

"I'm so sorry for what I did. All of it. I made it worse instead of better. I just want it to be over. Please, finish with this. We need to get on with our lives." She slumped back into her chair and wrapped her arms around herself.

Hélène looked sympathetic. "We all want it to be over," she said. "But this makes it more complicated. Now I'm going to have to ask you to come down to the station and give us a statement."

Lisa looked up, terrified. "You're arresting me?"

Hélène gave her a patient smile. "No, no. If I was arresting you, I'd be taking you away in handcuffs. We just need to officially record your statement about the fingerprints we found and what you told me about the gun. We have an obligation to complete a thorough investigation and report on all the evidence we find."

She hesitated before adding to the burden on Lisa. "We also have some more questions related to your mother's murder and the gun used there. I know you want to help us on that too. That's all. You're not under arrest for anything."

They both heard the silent *yet* that hung in the air.

"We know you want to co-operate and help us solve

both these cases. I'm just making a request for you to come to the station and give us your statement. Would tomorrow morning at 9:30 be all right for you?"

Lisa still looked concerned. "Just a short conversation, right?"

"Well, it will be a formal statement for the record," said Hélène. "I'll be there to help you through it, but another detective will do the interview and the paperwork." She gave Lisa a reassuring smile.

Lisa took a slow steadying breath and put on a brave face. "All right, tomorrow morning's fine."

43.

It was a comfortable, warm summer day in the normally hot, humid and uncomfortable weather of Montreal in August. Dale and Susan were lounging at the picnic table on the patio in their back yard, watching the kids kick a soccer ball around on the lawn. Dale reached for his glass of lemonade and said, "They're going to be happy with their stay at camp next week. It'll be a good chance to meet some new friends and get away from the city for some outdoor fun on the lake and in the woods. Kind of like us playing in the bush, back when we were kids in the Kootenays."

"Even better without any bears back in the trees looking at *them* for lunch."

"Yeah, they'll miss that part of the fun, I hope." He laughed.

They were remembering their own childhoods, growing up in separate but similar small towns in southeastern British Columbia—industrial towns nestled in the mountains with lots of bears and other wildlife back among the trees. Those childhood experiences were very different from those of their children being raised in the buzzing multicultural metropolis of Montreal. For Sean and Keira, two weeks at camp in the Laurentian Mountains north of the city would give them a brief experience of the natural environment that their parents had grown up in.

They looked over at the kids as the soccer ball banged off the fence behind Sean. Keira pranced away across the lawn, chanting, "I'm the winner-r-r! Yahoo!"

Sean yelled after her, "We're not done yet! It's your turn in goal now." He pointed at the space along the fence between two flowering bushes.

"No problem," said Keira, "the shutout continues." She backed into the space and crouched forward with her arms dangling, palms up, ready to block the shot.

Dale laughed at the scene. "I think they're due for a change at camp, alright. It'll be good for us, too, a little more time to ourselves with some peace and quiet."

"You maybe need the peace and quiet," said Susan. "I'm anxious to get back in action again. I hope you've got some work for me at the office. I need a change from the long, boring sessions of cancer treatment and the physio during recovery. It's been good to get back in shape and a little strain on the brain will be good for me too."

"No problem. We've got lots of work for you at the office. Marie will be happy to offload a ton. It might not strain your brain very much doing paperwork, so I'll try to find something more stimulating for you. Actually, I'll get you to review my revised marketing and sales plans. Our new marketing material, ads and posters, too. You're good at that stuff."

"I'm looking forward to it. How're you doing in your joint venture with Jean-Guy at Phoenix Systems?"

"Great. He's a really smart guy and a good manager

who knows his stuff. His team is very capable too. They've been training our staff on sales tactics and the selling points for our new product lines."

"So business is good then. The bank is impressed?"

"Well, I'm never satisfied and the bank is hard to impress, but essentially, yes. We're getting back on track and doing well financially again. That's a big relief, but it's no time to get complacent about it. We still have to work hard and be smart about the moves we make. It'll be interesting to hear what you think about our plans going forward. You always have some different ideas for me to think about. And you're not exactly a disinterested spectator. If it's good for the business, it's good for the family too."

"And what about the other stuff that's been on your mind, the death of Bobbie Brydon and then the murder of Donna?"

"I don't have any news on that subject lately. I'm just happy to be left out of it, actually. I've got enough to do. But I'm seeing Frank next week and he'll probably have an update for me. I know Hélène and her detectives are still working on it. They still think Bobbie's death was suspicious and Donna's might have been a Mafia revenge killing, apparently. It's all complicated by their connections to the Luciano family, who have a violent history in organised crime."

The were startled from their thoughts of Mafia murders by another bang as the soccer ball bounced off the fence on the far side of the lawn. Sean raised his arms and strutted around the lawn this time. "Hah!" he said. "No more shutout. Who's the winner now?"

Susan called out, "All right, you two. That's enough soccer practice. Go inside and wash up for lunch. I'll bring it out here and we can eat in a few minutes."

Keira was not happy to settle for a tie. She kicked the ball into the corner and it rolled up against a tall row of white hydrangea. "Hey, don't wreck my flower beds," Susan called out.

"Sorry, Mom," said Keira and she raised her hands in apology. She ran over to pick up the ball and placed it on the top step by the back door before heading into the house behind Sean.

44.

Claude was being coached by Hélène to take a hard line in the recorded interview with Lisa. He still looked reluctant to take that approach. "It was easier to be tough on her mother," said Claude. "She was a hard-ass bitch and didn't deserve any sympathy. But Lisa? I think you're trying too hard to find something that isn't there, Hélène."

"Well, she finally told the truth about her gun," said Hélène. "And maybe it's not the whole truth. I got something out of her with my kind and gentle approach, but I need you to push her again with your own hard-ass questions, Claude. Maybe she'll cough up something else. Fake it if you have to."

"Don't worry, I never have to fake it. I might even push a little harder than you'd like, maybe lose it a little, but I'll get whatever she's hiding. If there's anything that she hasn't told us yet."

They got up to leave Hélène's office and she said, "I'll bring her into the interview room, go through the preliminaries, and get her set up so she's relaxed and comfortable. You can wait behind the glass, then come in with both barrels blazing when you're ready."

Claude nodded and clenched his jaw. He assumed the look and posture of a determined detective as he strode down the hallway toward the dimly lit room that provided a view through one-way glass into the interview room. A few minutes later, Hélène was seated across from Lisa at the metal table in the middle of the room. A microphone sat on a low tripod between them for the interview. Hélène collected the few completed forms that Lisa had signed to allow the recording to proceed and a transcript to be prepared for the case files.

"I have no new questions for you," said Hélène. "Detective Claude Samson will conduct the interview. He'll be here shortly, and I'll remain as a witness. Any questions before we start?"

Lisa shook her head and lowered her eyes to the copies of the signed paperwork that Hélène had pushed back for her to keep. They sat quietly, preoccupied with their thoughts, when they were startled by the door opening brusquely and Claude Samson strode into the room.

He dropped his files on the table before pulling up a chair beside Hélène. He acknowledged Hélène with a nod, then turned to face Lisa and moved closer to the table and filled her field of view, leaning forward with his elbows on the table and his hands clasped on the pile of file folders.

"Lisa Brydon," said Claude, checking that the red light flashed on the microphone placed between them. "Thank you for giving us your statement and coming in today to answer our questions during this recorded interview." He stated the date and time and introduced himself by title, precinct and badge number, then continued.

"You have told us that the gun we found by your

father's body at the offices of 3D Computer Products on May third, 1993, was in fact, a gun that you had given to him. But you never admitted that it was your gun, until we advised you that your fingerprints were discovered on the bullets with the gun. Is that correct?"

Lisa nodded. Claude pointed at the microphone, and she said, "Yes."

Claude continued. "Now, I'm telling you we have found the gun that killed your mother and it also has your fingerprints on it. How do you explain that?"

Lisa was jolted up straight. "What? No way! Impossible. How did you find it? You have no search warrant."

She stopped herself, recovered her composure, and peered at Detective Claude Samson. "You're lying. You don't have that gun."

"That's an interesting reaction," said Claude. He glanced up from the microphone to the camera in the corner behind him. "That won't look so good on the recording when they see it in court."

Lisa leaned forward and shouted at him, "You lied to trick me! You can't do that. It's called entrapment. It proves nothing."

Claude didn't blink. "So where did you hide the gun?"

"I don't have the fucking gun!" Lisa tossed her hands in the air and leaned back in her chair. She looked at Hélène and sneered, "You set this up, you sneaky bitch. I've got nothing more to say to either of you. You've got more questions, talk to my lawyer."

Claude was not deterred. "But we know that you got two guns from your Uncle Tony's hit man, Vinnie Mancuso."

"He's not a hit man!" She calmed herself and folded her arms across her chest. "But yes, he gave me a gun and one for my mom, too. He knows guns. It was for our protection."

"Well, this is what I think," said Claude. "I think you wanted protection from losing everything while your parents were fighting over it. You used one gun on your father, just walked into his office and shot him in the head. Tried to make it look like a suicide. You thought you'd get your money, but your mother decided she'd keep it all to herself. Your best solution then was to kill her too, so you'd get it all."

He paused to let his account sink in. "Your mother never got the gun from you to protect herself. You kept it, and when you got the chance you walked into her house and used it on her. Three shots in the chest." Claude leaned back in his chair and crossed his arms above his belly to wait for Lisa's response.

Lisa scowled at him for a moment, then dismissed him with a toss of her head and turned to Hélène. "Are you believing this bullshit?"

Hélène did not respond.

"You're both living in fantasy land," said Lisa. "You have nothing. Maybe some fabricated circumstantial evidence. You think you can charge me with two murders? You have nothing. I know about the two guns, but somebody else could have used them. Maybe I lost them both. Maybe I gave them back to Vinnie. My defense is easy, your case is a joke. I'm out of here."

She pushed the chair back as she stood up, then leaned forward with her hands on the table to face them both. She turned to Hélène with a cold glare and said, "You have the cuffs for me this time?"

Claude replied, "You're not going anywhere. You'll be spending the night in jail. You should get used to it. You'll be there for a long time after we convict you of two murders. Not much mercy or forgiveness for somebody who kills both their parents."

"Bullshit!" Lisa slammed the chair against the table. "No way! I'm calling Uncle Tony. He knows how to get me out of here. Get me to a phone."

The two detectives remained seated.

Claude said, "Don't count on him. Tony already thinks you tried to set him up for killing your parents."

45.

"Thanks for taking me out to lunch at Lafleur's," said Dale. "Great hot dogs and fries, and it doesn't break the bank." He was sitting with Frank in the Cadillac in the large paved parking lot at Lafleur's Drive-in Restaurant off the service road near Pierre Elliott Trudeau airport. There was the usual mix of truckers and taxi drivers, businessmen and office workers, all sitting in their vehicles or lounging at the picnic tables in the warm sunshine, enjoying a quick lunch at their favourite hotdog stand. Dale and Frank had their seats moved back, each with a box of all-dressed hotdogs and fries open in their laps and soft drinks in the cup holders between them.

Frank nodded. "Well, business is not that good for me these days. Not enough serious crime to keep me earning big fees from anybody. And you're not paying me anything, as usual. I need to be careful how I spend my money," said Frank. "Not making my next million in the computer business and spending it on fine dining like you."

"I'd like to pay you more, Frank, but business is not that good for me either. I've stopped going backwards, I think, but no fine dining yet. You'll have to wait a while for the fine dining establishments you really like. Meanwhile, we'll have to settle for this."

He stabbed a couple of fries and dipped them into the

dollop of ketchup he'd squirted from the dispenser at the counter into the box and raised them with his plastic fork. "Best fries in town." They disappeared into his mouth, and he patted his lips with the brown paper serviette. "So, you're not busy enough, not having fun, and not making money dancing between the Mafia and your girlfriend, the super cop, who's trying to put them in jail."

"You make it sound more exciting than it really is," said Frank. "The crime business is pretty slow these days. I may have to go back to working for angry women trying to catch their husbands misbehaving. The divorce business is booming."

"How's Hélène doing in the crime business? Has she solved the Brydon murder cases yet?

"She's going around in circles, I think. Not much luck finding any proof of murder or who did it. She got nothing from the Lucianos. She even tried pushing Lisa to admit something, but that just made her shut down too."

"Lisa? I thought she was co-operating with Hélène. They're not accusing *her* of something now, are they?" Dale reached for his Coke and frowned at the idea of Lisa being involved in her parents' deaths.

Frank nodded slowly and replied, "It got complicated when they found her prints on the gun that killed Bobbie Brydon and she also may have been in possession of the gun that killed her mother. She got both guns from your friend, Vinnie Mancuso."

"Never my friend, Mancuso. Maybe it was your friend,

Tony Luciano."

"That's a good question. And did she really want the guns for protection or for murder?"

"No way she's capable of murder, She's a bright, strong young lady, but she's not evil. She might have a temper like her dad, and be a wicked schemer like her mother, but she's not a murderer."

"Sounds like a murderer to me, but you might be a good character reference for her if she needs one."

"What are you talking about? Has she been charged already?" Dale took a mouthful of Coke.

Frank said, "I don't have the latest. Hélène and Claude are trying to build the case that she killed both her parents, but they don't have proof yet and Uncle Tony got her a get-out-of-jail-free card. She wouldn't admit to anything except that the gun used on Bobbie Brydon was hers. They think she was desperate to protect her lifestyle and tired of watching her parents fighting over the money and pissing it all away. Angry, armed, and dangerous—she decided to look after herself by killing her father in a fake suicide, then making the murder of her mother look like a Mafia hit. She was doing a pretty good job of covering it up and directing suspicion at everybody else—including you, her mother, her Uncle Tony, and Vinnie Mancuso. Problem is, she won't admit to anything, and they can't prove a thing."

Dale sat back and gazed out through the windshield.

"Wow. That's hard to believe. She sure fooled me, if any of it's true. I thought I knew her pretty well. It just doesn't seem possible for Lisa to do all that. Her mother, yes. Not Lisa. I'd say it's more likely Donna had Tony kill Bobbie, then he had to shut her up about it when she started defending herself to the police. Tony's the one getting away with murder, not Lisa."

He was shaking his head and trying to think of another plausible explanation. "So, what happens now?"

"I don't know," said Frank. "I've got nothing that helps anybody, we can't prove anything. How about you? Are you ready to confess, like Tony Luciano wanted? Then we could all wrap it up."

"Nope, not me. I'm staying out of it," said Dale. "I've got nothing that helps anybody, either. I don't see any way Lisa can be their best suspect, but I don't really have a better idea."

"I don't think you're going to be lucky enough to stay out of it. They all think you've got more to tell—Hélène, Lisa, and Tony Luciano too. It's just a question of who'll call on you next."

Dale clenched the paper napkin into a ball and dropped it into the box on top of the few remaining fries. "Jeez, thanks, Frank. Now you've spoiled my lunch." He closed the box on his lap and brought his seat forward. "You can drop me back at the office and I'll try to get my mind back on business again. And not worry about who's coming to visit."

46.

Late in the evening, Dale's BMW sat alone in the dark in the parking lot at 3D Computers. Traffic on the TransCanada highway and the service road were relatively quiet. Inside, lights were on in the reception area, down the front hallway, and in Dale's office. There was no noticeable activity in the building. Dale was in his office, again lost in thought.

Things were going so well not long ago, what the hell happened? How did I arrive here? I nearly lost everything, and now, in the middle of it all, I have to worry about fending off the police and the Mafia too.

I've already had to fight off nervous creditors and the bank, layoff people and reorganise the business. I think I've avoided the crash landing, but how did I not see it coming? Too complacent, not paying attention? Too busy patting myself on the back for being such a big shot? Arrogant and over-confident? That's a helluva combination.

Maybe I was distracted by the family drama. At least we got past that.

There are no good excuses. Big mistakes always cost money. Sometimes they can cost you your business. But I turned it around. It could have been a complete fucking disaster. I wish I'd done a better job. I avoided the worst, and the good times are coming back, but I hurt a lot of people in the process. I'm never making those mistakes again.

He was unaware of a red Porsche that approached from the west and slowed at the driveway entrance into the parking lot at 3D Computers before turning in and driving past the front door to park out of sight at the side of the building. A slim young woman got out wearing a fashionable track suit and running shoes. She looked around the empty parking lot in front of 3D Computers and pulled a hoodie up over her blonde hair. Her face was not visible to the lights or the security cameras on the corners of the building.

She walked up to the entrance door and pulled it gently to confirm it was closed and locked. She continued along the front of the building and tapped on the window of Dale's office with her car keys. She leaned forward to put her face near the glass and look in on him.

Dale turned toward the tapping at his window and saw Lisa looking in and gesturing for him to go to the front door. He frowned, then got up from his desk and left his office to go down the hall and through reception to open the door.

"Lisa, what are you doing here?"

"Dale, we have to talk. I need your help."

"Now? I'm here just a little while longer before I go home. I don't think there's much I can do for you, Lisa. Let's arrange to meet another time if you really want to talk to me."

"It's urgent. It has to be now."

Dale wasn't convinced, but he stepped back and let

her in. "I'm sorry to hear you're still mixed up in all this," he said. "I heard about the charges against you, but really, there's nothing I can do to help."

"Let's go down to your office and talk about it," said Lisa.

Dale noticed she had her right hand jammed in the pocket of her track-suit jacket and the hoodie still pulled over her head. She gestured with her left hand for Dale to go first, back down the hall to his office. Dale glanced down the quiet hall to his left on the way past. There was an office door open and the light was on. He continued toward his own office and stepped quickly in. He went to sit behind his desk and indicated the chair in front for Lisa.

She pushed the hoodie back off her head and smirked.

"This not a social call, Dale, and we don't really have to talk."

She pulled her hand out of her pocket holding a large calibre revolver and pointed it at Dale. "I'm here to solve that problem we've been talking about. I'm not going to jail because of you!"

Dale stood and held his hands out, as if pushing Lisa away. "Wait a minute, Lisa. Please, put the gun down. I don't know what you're talking about, but the gun is not going to solve anything."

Lisa yelled louder. "Uncle Tony was right! You're the problem. We don't want you talking to the police anymore!" She poked the gun toward Dale across his desk. It wobbled in her hand, but it looked dangerously lethal and Dale couldn't take his eyes off it.

Lisa ranted, "You've been the problem all along. You're the one who could have saved my dad's business in the first place. You could have come up with the money when his company was in trouble, but you refused. Then you tried to take advantage of him, and you took advantage of me too! Trying to fix your fucking business. We had our own problems and you were supposed to help!"

Dale tried to stay calm. He looked past Lisa at the open door to his office. He raised his own voice. "Lisa, please! I don't know what you're talking about. I tried to work with you and your dad to help you out. I'm still trying to do that. Please, put the gun down. Then we can talk about it."

"We've had enough of your help, Mr. Hunter. You don't like the gun?"

She held it sideways to look at it herself. "You were here when my dad was shot. You should know better than to work alone in the office at night."

"He's not alone."

They both heard Susan's voice from the door.

Lisa stepped back and Susan saw the gun. Lisa reached for her and grabbed her arm to pull her into the office, holding the gun against her ribs. She pushed her up against the chair in front of Dale's desk. Dale was now more alarmed with the gun pointing at Susan but tried to remain calm.

"What are you doing, Lisa? What do you want from us? You're already in enough trouble. You're accused of killing your parents."

"Of course I killed them!" Lisa roared with laughter, and her wild eyes flashed as she pushed Susan up toward the front of Dale's desk and stepped back out of reach.

"And I'm going to get away with it!"

She waved the gun back and forth at Dale standing behind his desk and at Susan standing in front of it. They were both transfixed as she continued her mad tirade.

"I'm even leaving the gun here. It's the one that killed my mother. Everybody's looking for it and they'll find it right here with your fingerprints on it."

She turned to look at Dale with evil eyes he had never seen before.

"I had a plan to use it on you. Just like I did with my dad. Another suicide at the office. Now I'll have to kill both of you since your lovely wife has decided joined us."

She gave Susan a cold, determined stare.

Dale looked at the gun in Lisa's hand—a large revolver with a short shiny barrel. She held it in both hands. It was not held steady.

She might not be able to aim and shoot quickly. But she's pointing it at my wife!

I'm further away. She needs to aim it at me and keep Susan out of the line of fire. Maybe she'll miss us both.

Dale shouted, "Lisa, listen to me! We can talk about this. We can help you. Don't make it worse." Lisa held Susan by one arm and the gun barrel moved in Dale's direction to point at his chest.

Maybe her aim is good enough to kill me from there. I

need to keep her talking.

Lisa laughed again. "It was going to be one more suicide, I know how to do that, right? Now it's even better, it'll be a murder-suicide. Who's going to be first?"

The evil eyes flashed from Dale to Susan and Lisa's face turned grim. "I think it's better for the angry wife to shoot her loser husband, then she'll kill herself. I think that works best."

"Lisa, that's ridiculous. Nobody's going to believe that."

Dale looked for a weapon he could use and saw only a pointed brass letter-opener with a leather handle and a heavy, brass paperweight on his desk. It had the shape of a maple leaf with deep, sharp edges along the sides.

Maybe I can grab it and throw it at her. I'll have to distract her from shooting first.

"Lisa, let's talk this through. We can help you save yourself."

"Fuck off! Stop talking! You know I can make it look like suicide and you know I'm capable of murder."

Dale was awed by her face of dark murderous determination.

"I learned a lot from Uncle Tony," she said. "How to get away with murder even." Her sinful smile twisted into an ugly snarl. "My parents were so fucked up … they're better off dead."

She paused and looked from Dale to Susan. The gun was waving back and forth. "I'm much better off without them." She laughed quietly to herself. "I think I'll join

Uncle Tony's family… he's more my style."

Dale moved back from the desk and started to slide to his left. He kept talking. "You'll never get away with this, Lisa. Please let us help, we can explain the pressure you were under. Maybe your dad's death was an accident."

"Shut up. Don't be stupid. Stand still!" She frowned in concentration and held the gun steady pointing it at Dale. "I have to make this look like Susan shot you first, then herself."

Lisa stepped forward to grip Susan's arm and push her closer to the desk. Dale looked at the two women standing in front of him—slim, blond, attractive young women about fifteen years apart in age, but eons apart in character and mental stability. Lisa was agitated, angry, and looked insane. Susan looked calm.

How the hell can she be calm?

Dale felt his pulse throbbing as Lisa swung the gun in his direction again. He waited for Lisa's eyes to move off of him and go back toward Susan. He snatched the heavy brass paper weight and ducked down to the floor behind the desk.

Lisa pointed the gun over the desk and yelled at him, "Dale! Get out of there!"

A loud gunshot shattered the silence and a bullet sliced through the space over his head. He lunged out from behind the desk to the side and rolled into a crouch with his arm raised to fling the brass missile at Lisa.

He looked up to aim it just as Susan knocked Lisa's arm

sideways and the gun fell to the floor. In one fast motion, Susan thrust her arm forward, then slammed her elbow back into Lisa's throat. Lisa collapsed to her knees, gagging and holding one hand to her throat, the other hand raised weakly toward Susan.

Susan shouted to Dale, "Get the gun!"

She pushed Lisa's hand aside and punched her hard in the face, momentarily pulled her hand back in pain, then threw Lisa face down on the floor, wrenched her arm behind her back and kneeled on top of her to hold her there. Lisa struggled briefly before relaxing into Susan's tight grip. She coughed and cursed, then lay still, flat on the floor with Susan kneeling into the small of her back.

Dale stepped forward to reach for the gun that lay on the floor beside them, then he stopped. *No fingerprints, just Lisa's this time.* He reached into his pants pocket and pulled out a white handkerchief that he placed over the revolver before picking it up cautiously. He went back behind his desk and placed the warm gun in the bottom right-side drawer. A wisp of smoke rose from the drawer as he pushed it shut.

He looked up at Susan and raised his eyebrows. "Where the hell did you learn to fight like that?"

She shrugged. "They had a bonus yoga class on self defense last year. Mostly to protect ourselves from male attackers with a knife. Apparently, it works on young ladies with a gun too."

"Apparently," said Dale.

Susan pushed the hammerlock tighter on Lisa and kneeled into her kidneys. "Don't move, you bitch. I'll kill you if necessary to protect my family."

Lisa moaned and lay still.

Dale was shaking his head at a Susan he'd never seen before. He lifted the desk phone to his ear and hit the buttons for 9-1-1.

"Don't do that yet," he said to Susan. "I'll get the police here right away to take her off your hands."

47.

Several weeks later, Dale was walking quickly down the steps from the provincial courthouse to Rue Notre Dame in Old Montreal when he heard a voice calling out to him. "Hey, Hunter, hold on a sec." He turned toward the familiar voice of the *Gazette* reporter, Robert Martinelli, who was following him down the steps. "How'd you enjoy your day in court?" he said.

"Sorry, no comment for you today, Robert, "he said. "It wasn't really my day in court anyway. It was Lisa Brydon's day. I was just there with my wife to give our version of events. She's already on her way home and I'm on my way back to the office. No time to chat. You should have enough to write about anyway if you listened to Lisa's court appearance today."

"No problem, I'm not looking for comments. You gave me enough to work with in your testimony with your wife. My article is already finished. You'll be in the news again in tomorrow's *Gazette*, but as the judge requested, we won't mention your names. I'd still like to talk to you, though, about the case against Lisa Brydon. Off the record and the coffee's on me. There's a Second Cup right there across the street." He tipped his head in that direction.

Dale paused on the bottom step. He was already heading for the Second Cup to grab a take-out café latté before he heard Martinelli behind him. He hesitated to consider the offer. "Fine, I've got time for a quick coffee. And I'd actually like to hear your professional opinion as an experienced crime reporter on what happened there in court today. Does the offer to buy me a coffee make me a paid informant now?"

"Not yet. And we never pay, only the police do that. I'm just offering a friendly coffee and a little conversation."

Once they were seated inside with their coffees, Dale said, "Alright, you first. Do you think Lisa Brydon is going to get away with murder?"

"I'd say your testimony and your wife's will help get her convicted. Maybe not sufficient proof for first-degree murder, perhaps some version of manslaughter on grounds of temporary insanity from the distress of her situation. She has some pretty creative lawyers on her side who are good at confusing a jury and persuading them to have doubts. Even with very credible witnesses like you and your wife telling them Lisa pretty much confessed to two murders while waving a gun at you and planning to do two more."

"Yeah, but I wish my wife wasn't included in today's testimony. Lisa and her Mafia gangster uncle, Tony Luciano, already wanted to kill us when she was first charged. I think he talked Lisa into coming after us. Now he'll be even more determined to shut us up."

"It's too late for them to do anything to silence you now. Your testimony is already on record."

"Yeah, that's what the lawyers told us. But I'm not

feeling that secure from Luciano. He has a reputation for settling scores. And I still think he was behind both murders. He somehow turned Lisa and maybe her mother into lethal weapons to do his dirty work."

Dale then looked up sharply and said, "For chrissake, don't print that. I don't need him to keep thinking I'm trying to take him down."

"Don't worry. He knows the whole world is trying to take him down and you're not his biggest threat. He needs to worry more about Lisa explaining that he was behind it all. She's capable of implicating him to protect herself. He may have to remove that risk the same way he might have done with her mother. The guy is ruthless. If anybody knows how to get away with murder, it's him."

"Jeez. I appreciate the coffee, but I really didn't need to hear that again. How do you expect me to ever feel safe from these guys?"

"You're as safe as any of us, Dale. Innocent bystanders or not, any one of us can get caught in the crossfire. Montreal is a great city, but it can be a dangerous place to live."

"It's a great place to live," said Dale. "Always interesting."

"Yeah right, interesting." Martinelli raised his coffee cup. "*Vive la ville de Montréal!* Sometimes a little too interesting, but lots of good material for us reporters."

Dale lifted his cup in reply. "Keep up the good work, Robert. But I don't want to see my name in the papers again any time soon."

"You never know, Dale. You never know."

They put their empty coffee cups on the counter on the way out and went back to the street to go their separate ways.

The End

THANK YOU & ACKNOWLEDGEMENTS

First and most importantly, thank you to all the readers who spent their time reading the novels in the Dale Hunter Series, then sharing the books and their commentary with other readers. Your loyal support and encouragement are very much appreciated.

All my novels and business books are inspired by real-life stories of the entrepreneurs and business associates I have worked with during the last forty years and more. I sincerely thank them for sharing their stories with me and hope they forgive me if they're not flattered by the characters that appear familiar, or they think I got the story wrong. Remember, it's fiction! Based on a few facts, my faulty memory, and a fertile imagination.

My writing and storytelling have improved along the way from the first novel to the last with the active support and feedback from early readers, reviewers, and editors, especially my fellow writers and friends and family who continually cheer me on and inspire me to get better. They offer more than polite compliments, they tell me what they really think. Then they recommend the books to their friends. For CRASH LANDING, I must add a special thank you to perceptive reader, Patricia Lavoie, for her valuable review comments and corrections on the final draft manuscript.

I have also had the benefit of outstanding professional support for the earlier novels in the Dale Hunter Series with helpful editing and coaching by Allister Thompson, Alan

Rinzler, and Anna Bierhaus. This novel had the additional benefit of critical editing and commentary from editors Jerry Shaw and Kenneth Zink. Any remaining deficiencies are entirely my responsibility. The creative work on book design and covers for the latest three novels in the series are by the talented team at Miblart. The complexities of publishing, printing, and distribution are handled by the professional services of IngramSpark, Amazon/KDP, and Rapido Press. For the final steps in delivering books to readers, I am most appreciative of the many dedicated booksellers locally and internationally who do the matchmaking of good books to interested readers.

I've found the writing and publishing of any book is a weird combination of a lonely marathon endurance race and a fiercely competitive team sport. It takes sustained efforts of talent and hard work from everyone contributing to the final results. I appreciate them all.

My novels have also been a fun family project, with inspiration and input, critique and commentary from my grandsons, Lucas and Michael, my children Kim and Jon, and my patient and loving wife, Penny Rankin. (Always fun for me, not always fun for them.)

Thank you all!

Del Chatterson

Montreal, Québec, Canada
July 2024

THE AUTHOR – DELVIN R. CHATTERSON

 Like Dale Hunter, Del Chatterson is an engineer from the University of British Columbia with an MBA from McGill, and he ran a computer products distribution business in Montreal in the 1980s. Some of the stories in the Dale Hunter Series actually happened, most are fiction. "These are my worst nightmares," he says. "that I decided to share through the novels."

Del started his own business, called TTX Computer Products, in 1986 and grew it to $20 million a year in sales with distribution centres in Montreal and Boston. He then took it into a merger to expand the business across Canada. The merger was a disaster and was soon wound up, as the computer industry rapidly evolved and became more concentrated around a few major players, squeezing out smaller businesses everywhere.

Del has shared his business expertise as a strategic advisor, consultant, coach, and cheerleader for enlightened entrepreneurs and he has written extensively on business topics for decades. In addition to continuing the Dale Hunter series of crime novels, and publishing 2020 editions of his two business books, *Don't Do It the Hard Way* and *The Complete Do-It-Yourself Guide to Business Plans*, Del continues writing regular articles and social media posts and he is working on several short story collections and other works of fiction.

Originally from the Rocky Mountains of British Columbia, Del has lived and worked for most of the past fifty years in the fascinating, multicultural, bilingual, French-Canadian city of Montreal. Del has assisted entrepreneurs around the world with volunteer consulting and financial support in developing economies and in indigenous communities. His life experience outside of business and writing includes running nine marathons after the age of fifty (not setting any records, but never being last) and running for member of Parliament in the 2000 Canadian federal election. (He came second, not last.)

You can learn more about Del at his author website: DelvinChatterson.com and more of his advice for entre-preneurs at: LearningEntrepreneurship.com. You may also follow him on Twitter, Facebook, Instagram, LinkedIn, or YouTube.

Thank you for sharing his books and providing your feedback, comments, and reviews. Del welcomes every opportunity to connect with his readers, fans and friends.

* * *

Read more of the Dale Hunter Thriller Series:

NO EASY MONEY - *You never win playing by the rules...* First in the series of Dale Hunter Crime Novels, an explosive mix of crime, cash and computers in the 1980s. Entrepreneurs face challenges every day. It's hard to be a hero. Dale Hunter is facing threats from the Montreal Mafia and dirty dealing by crooked business associates. He wants to survive and not play by gangster rules. It will require courage and creativity and the support of some new friends. Somebody is going to get killed.

(See the short excerpt that follows.)

SIMPLY THE BEST - *It may be simple, it's never easy* Dale Hunter is again up against the gangsters who tried to murder him once and are now threatening his family. Meanwhile, Hunter's new partner in Taiwan is dragging him into smuggling schemes with the Triads. The danger escalates. Hunter's escape may be simple, but it's never easy.

MERGER MANIAC - *Some offers have to be refused* Dale Hunter is trying to save his business from competitive threats in the rapidly evolving computer business of the 1980s. He's looking for partners when he's suddenly approached by the Mafia to participate in their money laundering schemes. Hunter has to walk a dangerous tightrope to avoid getting dragged into more crime and corruption.

BAD BOYS IN BOSTON - *It's just business, never personal* Thirty years after fighting crime and corruption in the 1980s, Dale Hunter and Frank the Fixer are now drawn into rescuing a niece kidnapped into sex trafficking and online pornography by Russian gangsters in Boston. Dale and Frank follow a treacherous trail into the dangerous and violent international sex trade that also exposes Frank's tragic family history in Africa and more violent threats closer to home in Montreal.

CRASH LANDING - *Public pressure, private pain* Dale Hunter is fighting to save his business from disaster, when his business associate is found dead in an apparent suicide. The police immediately report it as a suspicious death, possibly murder. They pursue a widening web of likely suspects, including Dale Hunter. Then connections to organised crime are revealed and it suddenly gets more complicated and more dangerous. The only way out is to find the truth before Hunter becomes the next victim.

WHATEVER IT TAKES – *Trust nobody* Dale Hunter is shocked to discover that his friend and longtime mentor and role model as a successful entrepreneur, is a completely ruthless, greedy and ambitious egotist, probably crooked, and possibly a murderer. Hunter is asked to help extricate his friend from the dirty deals with criminals manipulating local politicians for profit in major municipal projects and instead of running for cover, Hunter gets drawn into the lethal conspiracies himself.

IN THE BEGINNING ....

DALE HUNTER AND FRANK THE FIXER WERE INTRODUCED

IN THE FIRST NOVEL OF THE DALE HUNTER SERIES.

FOLLOWING IS A SHORT EXCERPT.

No Easy Money

"YOU NEVER WIN PLAYING BY THE RULES."

LOOKING BACK

MONEY FOR NOTHING AND THE CHICKS ARE FREE

Dale Hunter was stuck in the continuous congestion of the Decarie Expressway driving toward downtown Montreal listening to the radio and that line was stuck in his head. It was the Dire Straits and their hit song, "Money for Nothing."

Dale was a fan. His favourite was "Sultans of Swing" with Mark Knopfler's long guitar solo at the end, though the damn DJs always let it fade out before the solo run was over. "Money for Nothing" reminded him of the 1980s and the computer business he owned back then.

But the money is never for nothing. Never has been for me anyway.

It was a hot humid day in July and Dale cursed himself for getting caught in the rush hour traffic. Now that he was retired, he should have been able to avoid it. He would rather have been cruising in his BMW-M4 with the top down along a winding road away from the city in the Laurentian Mountains. Instead, he was jammed into a pack of Montreal drivers with the top up and the windows closed, the air conditioning straining to shut out the heat, noise and pollution of the six-lane concrete trench known as the Decarie. It was always a stressful drive, so the music was a useful distraction and listening to the old favourites was added relief.

Dale's mind wandered back thirty years, to the time when Dire Straits first recorded those hits and he was a young entrepreneur riding high on the wave of personal computers that were flooding across North America. He smiled at the memories.

Then he remembered the first time that Jacques Talbot walked into his office and life became more difficult and more dangerous. The smile faded.

Talk about money for nothing.

1.

It was a cold winter day in January 1986, the day after the Space Shuttle Challenger had exploded immediately after take-off from Cape Canaveral, killing all seven astronauts. Everyone was talking about it. The TV images of shocked spectators looking up at the lingering brown plumes of smoke drifting away against a clear blue sky would be etched into their memories forever.

Dale Hunter was in his office in Montreal working on his own launch for a new line of computer products. He was writing up the promotions and product announcements to give to his sales team at 3D Computer Products.

Lost in thought staring at the computer screen, he was interrupted by his receptionist, Marie de Carlo, as she stepped into his office.

"Dale," she said, "there's somebody here to see you about insurance."

"Insurance?" He didn't turn from his keyboard. "I don't need to see anybody about insurance."

He heard a deep French-Canadian man's voice. "But Mr. Hunter, this is a very special kind of insurance. I'm sure it will be good for your business."

The voice was coming from the doorway behind his startled receptionist. Dale looked up to see a heavy-set man in a grey suit, no tie. An unfriendly face with an insincere smile. His hair was slicked straight back and down to his collar. Shiny black biker boots with rubber soles had allowed him to silently follow Marie down the hall.

"Thank you, miss," he said, as he squeezed by her, stepped into the office and reached out to Dale for a firm handshake.

He took a chair and pulled it up close to Dale's desk. Marie disappeared back down the hallway.

"My name is Jacques."

Dale took another look at him. *No last name, no business card? Not your typical insurance salesman.*

His suit fit tightly around heavy arms and shoulders. A burgundy silk shirt exposed gold chains at his neck and was stretched tightly over his round belly. *La grosse bedaine* as they say in Quebec. *If I ever have a big belly like that*, thought Dale, *please just shoot me.*

"I really don't need any insurance," Dale said. "We're well covered and I don't have time right now to hear your pitch. Leave me your card and I'll call if I'm interested. Thanks anyway, but I don't want to waste your time, or mine."

"Mr. Hunter," Jacques said, as he leaned forward holding the thin smile. "You don't seem to realize, this is insurance you absolutely must have. It's not really negotiable."

"Not negotiable… How's that?"

"Well, if you do business with us, we guarantee that certain types of accidents will just never happen." Jacques's smile disappeared and his eyes turned dark and menacing.

"And if you *don't* pay our insurance, we can promise you *will* have an accident. Either here or at home." He sat back and let it sink in.

"Jesus! You're looking for protection money?"

"We prefer to call it insurance."

Dale's mind raced and his stomach clenched as a cold chill ran down his back. He jumped up and pointed at the door.

"Get the fuck out of here or I'm calling the cops, right now!"

Jacques looked up, not moving from the chair. The smile returned. He continued, speaking slowly and firmly. "That's never a good idea. Our insurance actually protects you better than the cops and we really don't want them interfering in our business. This arrangement is just between you and me."

"We don't have an arrangement. So just get out of here, now!"

Jacques ignored him and continued.

"If I hear anything about cops, two things will happen. First, we'll show you the kind of accident that we're protecting you from, and second, your insurance will double from one thousand a week to two."

"No bloody way!"

"Look, I know you weren't expecting me today, so I'll give you some time to get used to it. I'll come back tomorrow afternoon. Just be sure you have an envelope ready for me. Mark it "Guaranteed Insurance" and put a thousand cash in it. Very simple. Got it?"

Dale glared at him and said nothing. Jacques got up and left the office.

Dale sat back stunned, then slammed his hand on the desk and exploded.

"Sonofabitch! Where the hell did he come from?"

Marie came back down the hall from her reception desk after Jacques went out the front door and looked in on Dale. "Everything all right?" she said. "Who was that guy?"

"Uh, yeah, no problem. Just another high-pressure salesman."

"Oh, OK." She went back to the front desk.

I need to have the cops here waiting for the sonofabitch when he comes back tomorrow. I need to stop this before it goes any further. Then Dale heard a crunch and the sound of broken glass coming from the parking lot.

He stood up and looked out to see a red Dodge RAM pickup backing away from the rear of his grey BMW coupe. The truck pulled forward to the curb alongside the building. Jacques got out and headed back in the front door.

He walked past Marie with a quick glance that froze her in place and went straight on to Dale's office. She watched him go down the aisle between the desks against the windows and the closed offices along the facing wall. One of the sales reps, Sylvie Cloutier, looked up from the paperwork on her desk and frowned as he went striding by.

Jacques went straight through Dale's doorway, walked over and leaned across the desk into Dale's face. "I had the feeling you might still be thinking about calling the cops."

He stood back with his hands on his hips and fingers below his belly. The grey suit jacket was pulled back like a gunslinger ready for a shoot-out. "I decided to give you a small demonstration of how we work. Just a broken tail-light this time. But if you ever go to the cops, we'll have to do more damage."

He stepped forward to put both hands on Dale's desk and leaned closer to him. "Remember, we know where you live and where your kids go to school. They're really cute in their little uniforms at Kirkland Academy. Don't give me a reason to run into them next time, instead of your car. Have the cash ready tomorrow."

Dale stared at him and sat still, trying to suppress the shudder that shook him in his chair.

"Just pay your insurance and I'll include child protection, no extra charge." Jacques smirked. "See you tomorrow." He turned and left again.

The back of Dale's neck tingled as he held his head in his hands, elbows on the desk. *This is for real.*

He reached out and absent-mindedly straightened the blotter to line it up with the front edge of his desk. Then he aligned the flat leather coaster with the top edge of the blotter. He got up and went to the door, closed it quietly, then paced slowly between the windows and the bookcase, circling the small conference table and two chairs. He paused to straighten a book on the shelf and stooped to arrange the papers more neatly in the blue recycling bin by his desk, then continued pacing.

It was a nervous habit. He was aware of it, but denied that he had what some people called OCD. "I'm neither obsessive nor compulsive and it's not a disorder," he explained. "I'm just trying to bring a little order into the chaos around me."

The visit from Jacques, demanding protection money and threatening his family, was going to be a challenge for him to bring into order.

* * *